I0630875

October Twilight

a Book of Short Fiction

by

Ron Terranova

REaDLIPS Press

Acquisitions: Rebecca Brooke & Jack Oddman, Jr.

Editor: Noreen Lace

Cover Art: Rocha

ISBN: 978-1-7331813-5-8
LCCN:

This book is dedicated to:

Noreen Lace
Daniel Felton and
Vivi Goenawan

Without their patience, technical expertise, and generosity, this book would not be possible.

Flip the calendar on its back. What do you see? Twelve months – twelve time intervals contained in twelve boxes?

I see a map. Twelve places, with distance boundaries, all with their own hues, landscapes and moods. I see time and place blended into realms, all sovereign, governed by their own rules.

My realm is October – the time and place where the wonderful co-exists with the sinister; where light and shadow engage in a dance of magic, dream and nightmare, and anything can happen, in day, night, or twilight.

This is where I live – October is my home.

TABLE OF CONTENTS

Reflexes Go Last

It was early March and Joshua had just turned twenty. He was taking the semester off to earn some money before going back to school. The gig at the sandwich shop was easy, and his boss would allow him to take a break whenever there were no customers. As a smoker, this was a valued perk.

Next door to the sandwich shop was a mid-rate hotel, and between the two buildings there was a makeshift patio area where people could relax and have a smoke. It was a small, shaded area that seemed to have been set up with deliberate poor taste. There were two round tables, both with two chairs, and a pair of reclining lounges. All the furniture was made of wicker and, off in the corner, there was the ludicrous head of some Tiki God.

It was late morning and, for the third day in a row, Joshua shared the patio with a guest from the hotel.

He was an older man, or so he appeared. He was in his sixties or even older, but when he stood up he looked tall and straight; his body lithe and fit. He was usually on the patio before Joshua arrived, laying back on a lounge with his feet crossed, looking completely relaxed as he slowly inhaled from a thin, black cigarillo. On this morning he looked at Joshua for the first time and smiled.

His grey eyes bore a weary kindness.

"How's the sandwich business, young man?"

It was the first time Joshua had heard him speak. "It's alright – steady enough for my boss to keep me on." Joshua tended to be wary of strangers, but somehow he felt completely at ease with this man.

Setting his cigarillo in an ashtray fashioned from a coconut, he extended his hand. "My name is John."

"My name is Joshua." The two shook hands.

John's grip was firm, and his smile sincere.

John picked up his cigarillo from the ashtray and stared at the cigarette in Joshua's hand. "Well, we share at least one vice," observed John. "It's funny how things change. When I was your age, everyone smoked. It was the thing to do. Now we're treated like pariahs. Why, I remember my dentist would have a cigarette dangling on his lips as he filled a cavity, and ashes fell into my mouth."

Joshua noticed a wry look of mischief on his new friend's face. Was he joking? It was hard to tell.

"So tell me Joshua, you're a college student, aren't you? Let me see if I can guess your major. Let's see – psychology?"

Joshua was taken aback. "Well, yes. How could you have known that?"

"Well, I could lie and say lucky guess, but there's more than luck. No one should ever depend on luck. I've been watching you the last few days, sometimes, through the corner of my eye as you deal with customers. I can tell from your expression and body language that you analyze and evaluate people's behavior. Am I correct?"

"Well, I guess – no, you're correct. I've always

been interested in what makes people tick."

John displayed that sly, good natured smile again. A mischievous smile, like that of a good humored leprechaun.

"You know, Joshua, I observe people as well, but within given contexts. Motives interest me. What drives them – what their behavior is, not so much in the long run but in the now. In my line of work if you don't have keen observational skills, you'll – well, the competition will get the upper hand and you'll fall to the wayside." John looked up at the sky. "So tell me, psychology major, are you familiar with a condition called synesthesia?"

"Well, no I'm not," he replied.

Still looking upward, John took a long drag on his smoke and continued. "It's a kind of perceptual blending. The most common form is to see as well as hear music. I have a form of this condition myself. For me, time and place overlap. As a child I could look at the back of a calendar, and I would see it as a map with the twelve months being separate places. October – now there's a place; I could live there forever. But this March we're in – it's like a climatic no man's land – no longer winter, but not quite spring. Everything looks grey or blanched. It's a month made for death."

"So what kind of work do you do, John?"

The wry smile returned. "Well, I'm an expeditor of sorts. An independent operator. When a company or concern hits the wall with an obstacle, I try to find a solution – a way around the wall. And if that doesn't work, a way to remove the wall altogether. You can't imagine the turmoil that results, and it's even harder to imagine the enemies a good expeditor makes. I tried retirement, but the idleness was a killer. I keep getting drawn back in."

Joshua reached for the ashtray on his chair's armrest and accidentally knocked it off. With amazing speed, John caught it before it hit the ground. "It's funny – so many things go to hell at my age, but somehow the reflexes go last."

Joshua glanced at his watch. Still too early for the lunch customers. He lit another cigarette and looked at John who appeared so calm, observing the world with a zen-like equanimity. Then, his eyes narrowed.

"Look across the street, Joshua. Look in front of the pizza place. Do you see that man getting out of the black van?"

Joshua looked. There was nothing extraordinary about the man except for his vest.

"Now Joshua, most people, yourself included,

would focus on that atrocious gold lamé vest he's wearing. But I know it's a diversion. Now if someone like that committed a crime, a witness would remember the vest to the exclusion of actual physical features. Now keep an eye on him. He's going to cross the street and walk toward us." As if on cue, the man crossed the street, looked around, and walked in their direction.

Joshua looked directly into John's face. The bemused smile was still there, but his eyes were cold and as grey as March.

"That man is here to kill me. But I have the upper hand. I know, but he doesn't know I know."

Joshua felt a chill – was this an expression of John's wry sense of humor – or maybe he was crazy?

"Stay or leave, Joshua. Your call. If he succeeds, he'll kill you next. Were it me, I'd leave – now."

Joshua tried to get off his chair, but he was drawn back. His fascination was morbid. It must be a joke. He had to see what unfolded.

The man in the vest paused, then continued, now just a few yards away. It was true about the vest; he couldn't take his eyes off it. It was like a glimmering shroud, concealing and defining the man who wore it.

Then, he closed in. Yes, it must be a joke. John remained placid, not moving an inch or changing expression.

The knife came out from behind the vest. John still seemed immobile, as if already dead.

The killer lunged. Somehow John was no longer in the chair. He was behind the killer; one arm around his neck, the other grabbing the knife. There was a sudden jerk of his wrist. The killer's throat opened, the gold vest now was tainted crimson.

The killer was on the ground, a red pool enveloping him. Joshua looked up – where was John?

He was gone, away from March, on his way back to October.

That Good Night

It began as a thought – a vague, whimsical notion.

It happened first when he was a young boy. He was not allowed to go outside by himself after dark. One night, after his parents had gone to bed, he awoke just before midnight. He sat up in bed and listened. It was so quiet he could hear the silence – the silence of the night.

His bed was beside a window and, on this warm October night, the curtain was drawn.

He looked outside at the backyard. He had lived all of his life in the large old house with his parents and grandfather, and he had played countless hours in the backyard. He knew every detail of the yard, every tree and shrub, the swing set and the tool shed. He could close his eyes and still see the yard and all it contained. But he had never truly looked at it after dark through his second floor bedroom window. He stared through the window for a long moment and was transfixed. It was the first time the thought came to him – the notion.

The following night he again awoke at the same time as the night before.

Making sure his parents and grandfather were asleep, he arose from bed and dressed. The thought was stronger than the night before.

He went downstairs, quiet as the night, and approached the back door.

He had to go outside. He felt compelled. His hand trembled slightly as he turned the doorknob.

He walked outside into the night. The thought grew stronger, and he stared in wonder.

It was barely discernable; only a keen eye could see it, but it was there. Night.

It was not a matter of looking at the same place that existed during daylight now shrouded in darkness. No – things were different, objects were different in size and shape and not located exactly as they were in daylight.

It was subtle; he could see how grown-ups with all of their worries and concerns would overlook what he saw. The differences were slight, almost insinuations that would be unseen by most – perhaps all except for himself. But it was there before him. A change – a shift in the way things were, undetected in the shadows of the night.

He felt a sudden chill, a fear that he knew a secret which no one should know. He ran back inside the house and returned to bed, covering his face beneath the warm sheets, blocking out the night.

He awoke to the bright glimmer of day. He pondered what he had seen the night before. The thought was still in his head. Should he speak of this? Who could he tell?

Grandpa.

Grandpa always seemed to understand him, his shifting moods and ways. When he would awaken from a bad dream, it was grandpa who would comfort and reassure him far more than his parents. "I know, I know," Grandpa would say. "I had bad dreams just like yours when I was a boy."

And so he and Grandpa found a quiet place, and he told him of the thought – the notion.

Was there a small shudder in his grandfather's face when he spoke of what he saw? Did grandfather also know the secret – the thought?

"No, no my boy," said his grandfather. "These are just thoughts. I had them too when I was your age, night thoughts. You mustn't think such thoughts. A young boy should think and live in daylight. Oh, the pleasures of day time. Think of sunshine and baseball, of running through the summer sprinklers, and listening for the happy ringing of the ice cream truck. The night is not for joy. It is a time for sleep. The more you think about night, the harder it is to stop." Then, his face became grave. He took his grandson close and whispered, "The night believes it is the way all things were meant to be – and that daytime is a mistake."

And so the boy heeded his grandfather. Grandpa was wise and understood the ways of life. It was difficult at first, almost an act of will. In bed, when darkness fell, he would draw the curtain over the window and sleep on his side facing the wall. During daylight, he did as his grandfather exhorted and learned to savor all that daytime had to offer. And as the seasons passed so did the years, and the thought grew distant in his memory.

He was now a young man, a recent graduate with a degree in architecture. He lived in a small town not too distant from his boyhood home and was establishing his career. He worked for a firm that specialized in custom homes and he became a favorite of his boss, who recognized his talents and doted on him like a son.

One of his talents was the ability to visualize a house before the blueprint had been drawn. He was able to work fast and with exceptional quality as he could see the finished structure in his mind's eye, and it was merely a matter of copying what he saw. He also had an uncanny ability to look at a space or object and know the size or dimensions without measuring.

One night after work, he realized he had left a set of blueprints at a building site where he had been conferring with the job supervisor. It was the only copy, and he felt compelled to drive the several miles back to the site to retrieve them.

When he arrived, he easily located the plans and placed them in the trunk of his car. As he was about to get in the car and drive back home, he stopped.

He turned around and closely observed the building site. The thought had returned.

The site *was* different from earlier in the day. The house was in the framing stage, and the dimensions seemed off; there was an almost imperceptible tilt to the frame. He looked at the area surrounding the site and, again, things appeared out of kilter: the lamp post, the fire hydrant, and the willow tree that was adjacent to the site. He could understand how those who never had the thought would be oblivious to the night change. It was subtle and nuanced, a wrinkle in the fabric of night, more of a tease than a provocation.

But surely a skeptic would say the frame is settling and the tree is in a constant state of flux, as are all trees, subject to the elements, growing and never truly inert. Perhaps it was time to test the thought.

He retrieved a tape measure from his car.

Starting with the fire hydrant, he measured its height and its distance to the edge of the curb. Then he taped the width of a cross beam within the frame. Yes, trees are always in some degree of flux, but they do not travel. He measured the distance of the tree's trunk to the fire hydrant.

The next day just after 11:00 a.m., he returned to the site and told the supervisor he needed to measure a few items to check the construction's conformity to the blueprints.

He started with the cross beam.

Last night, it was twelve and three quarter

inches wide. Today, it was twelve and two thirds. Next was the fire hydrant: At night, it was exactly three feet high; now, it was two feet and five sevenths of a foot.

The distance from the tree's base to the fire hydrant had been seventeen and five eights of a foot. Now it was seventeen and one half feet. Although his measuring ability was exceptional, he measured all items again with a different tape and got the same results.

He took the rest of the day off and went home to think.

Should he discuss any of this? Should he share the notion – the thought with others? They would think him mad, especially if he asked them to do measurements of the same objects at night, then at daytime.

Or, perhaps he should ignore the night changes and go about his daily business – his life. He had repressed the thought for many years since childhood and nothing dire had occurred. And yet…

The following night, he went for a walk around his block. Again, that subtlety of difference. He stared into the night and felt the night was staring back. It was as if the night had its own mind and point of view.

On this night, he noticed something new. He had walked around the block countless times on ground that seemed level, but now he felt he was walking on a very gradual incline uphill. He felt compelled once again to test his perception.

He returned home and retrieved from his garage two stakes, a spool of string, a hammer, and his tape measure. Walking back to the spot where he noticed the incline, he pounded a stake in the grass adjacent to the sidewalk and tied string on the top of the stake. Then, he walked about twenty feet ahead and pounded another stake into the ground and tied the other end of the string to it.

He measured beneath the first stake, and then measured beneath the second. The string was four inches higher beneath the second stake.

The following day was Saturday, and he was not distracted by work. He waited until 11:30, when the day was about to reach its apex, and walked to where the stakes had been placed.

He measured below the string, first one end, then the other. The ground was level.

He began to do research online and in libraries. Had anyone at any time observed the same phenomenon he had? He searched for something – anything – that even remotely resembled his experience: astrophysical causes; gravitational variations; climate change. Nothing. He researched the varieties of delusions described in the psychiatric publications and texts. Nothing. He changed course from the sciences and researched the great religions, desperate to find something, some mad saint or prophet who knew of the thought and saw the true nature of night.

Nothing. He was alone.

What had his grandfather said? "The night believes it is the way all things were meant to be – and that daytime is a mistake."

What if it were true – that daytime was the imposter and all of humanity dwelled since the beginning within a bubble of delusion?

It was a warm October night, just as it had been when the thought first came to him as a boy.

He awoke just before midnight and dressed himself. The thought was within his head, but with more insistence and resonance than ever. It grew and became dominant, subordinating all other thoughts, leaving him single minded.

He walked outside, gazing into the night.

All of his previous walks were circular, walks around the block, repeating the steps and sights within the circle. Tonight, he would walk straight ahead.

With each step forward, he knew it was real. What was flat ground hours ago, masquerading beneath the shroud of light, now was an uphill incline. Trees, signs, lamp posts appeared bent and twisted, vertical objects from day now leaned horizontal, some undulating with the October wind. Why – why did this not seem strange to him?

He continued walking – what was that ahead? It was an area, enclosed within a contorted wrought iron fence. He pressed forward and passed through an open gate. He was surrounded by odd shaped stones, slanted and misshapen. He was in a cemetery.

He pressed on, surrounded by a sea of surreal, grotesque headstones, and walked toward the rear gate. As he left the cemetery, he glanced at one of the headstones. It was toppled and appeared distorted, as if seen through a prism. It bore an inscription, barely legible. The words were familiar to him – he had seen those words before.

"Do not go gentle into that
good night – rage, rage
against the dying of the light."

He kept walking, intrepid and without fear.

The thought had left him.

He walked, without falter; with
every step, he grew closer, until he arrived
– and all was night.

Religion

David was searching for something, and he was losing faith he'd ever find it. He was searching for religion.

He was raised Catholic, but renounced the church at an early age. The priests were harsh and the nuns were worse. During confession, he felt he was locked inside a coffin with the silhouette of a wrathful priest glaring at him through a porous screen. The holy trinity, as far as he could tell, was guilt, fear, and shame. Why feel guilt and shame when he did nothing wrong? Fear was another matter.

He had sampled them all – or nearly so:

Buddhism, Hinduism, Judaism, Islam – but none of them resonated with him.

He was a junior in college, majoring in history and, on this bright October day, he was between classes, sitting on a bench and watching the trees dance like dervishes in the autumn wind – the devil winds of October.

A young man who seemed to appear from the shadows sat next to him. "Hey, mind if I join you?"

The young man had long hair, dark as night. David's hair was also long, but blonde with reddish streaks. The sun beams refracted from the strands and seemed to move with the wind.

The young dark haired man extended his hand. "My name's Jason." There was a pleasantness about him, an open and honest fraternal quality to his demeanor.

"My name's David." The two shook hands – Jason was a stranger, but David felt, somewhere and somehow, they knew one another. Ordinarily a loner who valued his solitude, there was an immediate sense of camaraderie with Jason.

"You're looking at the wind," observed Jason. "The wind and the trees. It's real special this time of year. Autumn is special – October in particular."

David looked at Jason – those eyes, almost black, the irises hidden in darkness. How could he know what he felt about the wind?

"Have we met before, Jason? You seem so – familiar."

"We haven't met formally – but you and I were in last semester's Comparative Religion class. I remember the questions you asked were the ones I would have asked, but you beat me to the punch." Jason stared at the wind buffeted trees. Then he looked at David. "Do you ever feel like everything is changing for the worse? Look at the climate – at Mother Earth. It's like we've lost our bearings and are adrift. Humanity has been led astray."

David nodded in agreement as Jason continued.

"Most people have been brainwashed by lying preachers and politicians. Take Sean Carlson for example."

"Tell me," replied David. "That bastard sickens me with his bible laced bigotry and stupidity. How did he get elected to congress? I hope the system was rigged, because I don't want to believe there are that many stupid, bigoted people to legitimately elect him. I try not to hate anyone, but…"

Jason interrupted, "Why do you try not to hate anyone? Some people deserve to be hated. If hatred inspires action, it can be positive." Jason leaned closer to David and whispered in his ear. "Long ago, before the Christians exiled the true gods, Carlson would be dealt with. And there would be no guilt – only joy."

"What – what are you saying, Jason?"

Jason moved closer to David and placed his hand on his shoulder. Ordinarily, David would feel uncomfortable with such unsolicited familiarity, but somehow not with Jason.

"Do you remember, David, when we discussed Pantheism and Animism in class? Once there were people who saw the higher power in nature – the people of the old ways." Jason himself seemed to grow animated, as if tapping into the higher power transmitted from the trees writhing with the wind. He smiled and continued. "These were the Pagans, David, and they're still here. You deal with them often, but you don't know it. They've gone underground."

David stared into Jason's face. He must have seen him before, before Comparative Religion class – they met, he felt, long, long ago.

Jason continued. "Long before the single God – the God of fear and guilt, the God who punishes us for taking pleasure and wanting freedom - there were many gods. We can still hear them. Moments ago, they spoke to us through the wind. We just have to learn to listen - to reconnect with our roots."

David was rapt. There had been times, like today, when he felt he was spoken to through the wind, rustling through the leaves with an ancient voice.

Jason clasped David's arm and drew him close. "David – the moon will be full and red tonight – blood red." His voice was nearly vibrating with excitement, a whisper about to become a roar. "I know these people David. The first full moon in October. Tonight is a holy night to Pagans. There will be a secret ceremony in a hidden place. I'm going – and I want you to come with me. You'll never regret it."

David felt a shudder of foreboding, which was superseded by his curiosity – and his growing excitement. "Well, alright Jason – you've persuaded me."

Jason was ecstatic. "Great!" It was more of a whoop than an exclamation. "Meet me at nine at the old clock tower on Dixon Street. The hidden place is not far from there."

It was nine and David stood below the clock

tower. The moon was aflame in the sky, almost surreal. It seemed to leer, like in pictures from children's books, swelling with each moment.

Jason arrived. "Let's go man! The hidden place is close by."

Jason was amused by David's obvious apprehension and could not help but to chuckle. "Relax David – I guarantee you'll love this – just like me!"

Jason led David to a thick grove of oaks on the outskirts of town. In the center of the grove was an amphitheater.

There were many people assembled - men and women wearing black robes. There was excitement and a joyous anticipation in the air.

There was an altar in front of the amphitheater illuminated by candles and a torch in the center. All about the assembly there were happy, excited murmurings. David had never experienced a place like this or people like the ones surrounding him. The energy they generated was raw and primal.

Then, a tall bearded man appeared behind the altar clad in crimson robes. Jason nudged David. "Be very still – this is the high priest."

"We are assembled here on this sacred night with the hallowed ground beneath us and the blood moon above. We rejoice! We live! They have tried to destroy us for millennia – we have been burned at the stake, hung from the gallows, and pressed to death with immense stones. We have been maligned, tortured, and hunted through the ages. But we will not be vanquished – we will not allow our gods to be annihilated, to be replaced by their one God – the false God. Tonight, we are not the hunted ones, but the hunters. And beneath the hunter's moon, we offer our prey to the true gods."

From behind the altar a struggling figure wearing a hood was dragged before the assembly. It was a man, semi-naked; a soft, obese man whose pale skin contrasted with the looming red orb in the sky.

David was nonplussed and frightened. What was happening? Was this a hoax? Some type of deranged performance art?

Jason grasped David's arm. "Just relax, David. The offering is the best part. I know you better than you know yourself – you're going to love this!"

The hood was wrenched away from the struggling man. David shuddered. It was Sean Carlson! He was gagged and his arms were bound behind his back. A look of horror and astonishment was frozen on his face.

Jason looked at David, amused by his new friend's bulging eyes.

"Suspend everything they ever told you, David." Jason's eyes and smile looked demonic. "You've been brainwashed, like all of us, and it's time for you to break free. You know what he stands for; everything you and I despise. This is justice, pure and direct, the way it was meant to be. Turn the other cheek? Love thy neighbor? That's what they've crammed down every slave's throat since the dawn of time."

The high priest stepped forward. Two powerful men, also clad in crimson robes, forced Carlson to his knees and placed his head on a thick, oaken block.

The high priest raised the scythe over his shoulder.

David's eyes bugged with shock. "What is this, Jason? Some sick joke? Take me out of here – get me away from these sick, crazy bastards!"

David tried to bolt, but his legs felt heavy and leaden.

Jason was ecstatic. "You'll see, David. You're just like me!"

The scythe came down. The assembly screamed with an otherworldly, primal joy.

The high priest raised the severed head and

began to chant. "Hail to thee, oh Mother of Night – hail to thee, Father, Lord of the Hunt – King of Vengeance."

The assembly stood with arms over head and chanted, "Hail to our Queen – Hail to our Lord!"

David's shock abated. He was transfixed. He felt as if a hood had been wrenched from his own head.

He felt power and ecstasy as he gazed at the severed head impaled on a pike. He knew what the wind had whispered as he inhaled the scent of fresh drawn blood beneath the glow of the hunter's moon. He knew the ancient truth and shuddered with the lust of the kill.

He began to chant, at one with the others – with Jason.

Then he raised his arms in triumph and began to howl.

Finally, he had found religion.

The Plunge

The high school pool had just been completed, and Ken Stearn's gym teacher, Mr. Eachus, wanted all of his boys to jump off the high dive.

He assembled his senior class and spoke. "Now I know all of you may have varying levels of skill and experience in swimming and, for some of you, dealing with heights may offer an additional challenge. What I want you to do is not so much about swimming and diving but about facing something you fear and overcoming it. This is one of the most important aspects of character, to face something you may dread and defeating it. To step up and forward and…" he paused and smiled paternally at the assembled young men, "and to take the plunge."

Mr Eachus then bent down with a length of rope and spread it between himself and his students. "Now, all of you who are willing to take the plunge step over this rope. For those who aren't up to it, let's talk about it. The plunge isn't scheduled till next week."

About fifteen of the twenty-one boys immediately stepped over. Five of the remaining six stood where they were, feet shuffling, heads bowed; then, they reluctantly stepped across. Only Ken Stearns did not step forward. "C'mon Stearns, don't be a pussy," an anonymous voice hooted from the crowd. "Yeah, come on man! You're the only one with no balls," jeered another. Then, he heard a familiar voice, from his best friend Sam. "Come on Stearnsy - I know you can do it." Ken and Sam had been friends since kindergarten. "Don't listen to these jerks - you've got more balls than all of them put together." One of the boys shoved Sam, and Sam shoved back.

"All right - all of you calm down and shut up. Class is dismissed!"

Mr. Eachus approached Ken. "Come on Ken. Let's go to my office and talk about this."

The two of them stepped into the office. Mr.

Eachus sat behind his desk and asked Ken to pull up a chair.

"What are you afraid of, Ken? I know you can swim. I've never seen you flinch or back down from the bullies."

Mr. Eachus paused and wiped some beads of sweat from his forehead. It was that time in October when Summer makes its final surge before the Autumn chill. The temperature was in the nineties.

"It's a hell of a thing about bullies," he continued. "They're like a jackal pack that gets bolder when they smell fear. They're not just in school; you'll be dealing with them all of your life like all decent people do."

Mr. Eachus looked at Ken. He had been his gym teacher all three years of high school. He felt a paternal attachment to the young man. He always sensed Ken was more sensitive and thought more deeply than most. But he also felt he had fine character and resolve.

"You gave the bullies in class a reason for boldness today. This isn't like you, Ken. The platform is sixteen feet high, not sixty. You jump, feet first, sink close to the bottom, then swim back up and get out of the pool. It will be over in seconds. And you'll have faced and overcome fear and shut the bullies' mouths."

Ken looked at his gym teacher. He had always looked up to him, almost as a father figure. He was sympathetic, but would he understand?

"I am afraid Mr. Eachus, but it's not the fear you may think. I've never been afraid of heights, and I'm a decent swimmer."

"Then what is it Ken? Do you fear hitting your head or blacking out? I'll be right there if you have any trouble, and so will your friends. Before I became a gym teacher, I was a lifeguard - and no one got taken by the big, bad ocean under my watch."

Ken swallowed and tried to find the words.

"I - I've had this dream since I was little - this nightmare. It's always the same. I'm looking down into a body of water. Sometimes it's the ocean, sometimes a lake - and sometimes a pool. And I'm surrounded by people who are screaming for me to jump. I'm being taunted and jeered because I hesitate. Finally, I give in to their taunts and jump. And as I descend the clear blue water changes to black - black like ink."

Mr Eachus listened with interest and sympathy. "And then what, Ken. What happens next?"

Ken's eyes widened as he answered, and his

brow began to tremble.

"I hit the water. It's a liquid void. And I sink - sink to a place that has no meaning - and no bottom. And I keep sinking, forever."

Mr. Eachus had listened intently to Ken's words. He evaluated and analyzed what was spoken. "Listen to me, Ken. This dark void, this bottomless pit and endless descent is the fear I've been speaking of. You and I know that what you've described is not rational. What you fear could never really happen; it would defy all of the laws of physics."

"I know, Mr. Eachus. And that's why it's so horrible - because it's irrational, because it's absurd."

"You have to break through this, Ken. Fear can cripple all of us for an entire lifetime. I want you to trust me on this. I give you my word - my pledge that you'll be fine after taking the plunge; you'll feel unburdened and liberated from this crazy notion that's festered inside your head for all these years."

Ken stared down at the desk. He felt trapped between two bleak choices: avoid the plunge and be looked upon as a coward and be haunted by the shadow of cowardice in other experiences and encounters in life, or take the plunge and either be freed from a life long dread or fall into something unknowable , dark, and endless. Then he raised his head. "Alright," he said, barely above a whisper. "I'll do it."

Mr. Eachus smiled with pride and embraced him in a paternal bear hug. "I'm proud - very proud of you Ken."

The day arrived. The temperature was still in the nineties, but Ken felt an icy chill.

The boys lined up in alphabetical order. Ken was fifth in line. To make the progression of turns fair, names were placed in a cap and drawn out randomly.

Steve Burns was first. He was one of the boys who had taunted Ken. He climbed the ladder to the platform, then stared down below.

"Nothing fancy, Burns. Feet first, body stiff," shouted Mr. Eachus. "That goes for all of you."

Ken looked up at Steve. He was no longer cocky. He saw fear in his eyes, and one leg nearly buckled. Then he jumped.

The splash sounded to Ken like a thunderclap. Almost immediately, Steve bobbed up and swam to the pool's edge.

"Good job, Steve," Mr. Eachus shouted.

A voice echoed in his head, "you should have landed on your gut and broken your ribs, you vicious little bastard."

Doug Horsky was next. He climbed up to the platform with an air of indifference. Without hesitation he made the jump, bobbed up, and was out of the pool, quickly and without ceremony.

Two more made the plunge without incident. Then it was Ken's turn.

All eyes were on him.

He walked slowly to the ladder and paused halfway up, then continued to the platform.

He walked to the edge, almost trance like. There was apprehension in his expression, but also something else - a look of resigned inevitability. And then he stood, immobile, like a statue on a pedestal.

Sam's voice rang out amidst the still, eerie silence. "Come on, Ken - I know you can do it - don't even think - just do it, man."

Then others joined in - even those who had mocked and insulted him previously.

There was solidarity - they all wanted him to succeed - to just get it over with and to move on.

Ken shivered for a moment, then was still. He called out.

"I'm counting on you guys," his voice shrill and cracking. It was more a plea than a statement.

"Mr. Eachus!"

"Yes. Yes, Ken. I'm right here. I won't let your fear take you."

"I'm counting on all of you - don't let me go away!" Then he jumped.

The collective cheer was deafening as his feet hit the water, his body straight and solid. Mr. Eachus was jubilant, sharing in Ken's triumph. "Yes! I knew you could do it - I knew it!"

Sam was equally elated. The grin on his face made his cheeks hurt. He stared at the pool's surface, ready to fist pump as his friend bobbed back up from below.

The splash from the impact had settled, and the pool water was level and passive.

Mr. Eachus felt a crawling dread inch up his spine. Where was Ken?

He ran to the pool's edge and looked down to the bottom. There was nothing. Then he dove into the pool, slicing through the water with practiced precision.

Two boys jumped into the middle of the pool as three others joined Mr. Eachus at the deep end. Sam dove into the middle of the pool.

When he opened his eyes, he saw Mr. Eachus flailing around wildly, his head turning in all directions. His eyes were wide with astonished panic.

The panic - the terror was spreading to Sam and the other boys. His eyes darted. Perhaps a dozen other boys had joined the frantic search. It was like an absurd human aquarium, people swimming and colliding in chaos.

Ken was nowhere to be found.

Mr. Eachus swam to the surface. His face was contorted with grief and disbelief. He took several deep breaths, then again dove below.

The boys had now surfaced, followed by Mr. Eachus. Everyone was shaken with incredulity. In unison, they all began to shout.

"Ken - Ken, where the hell are you?" screamed Sam.

Mr. Eachus was trembling. It was a joke - that's what it is, he thought. This was Ken's way of getting back at the taunting bullies, and at himself for lecturing him about fear and courage. That sneaky little prick, he thought. He must have figured a way out without being seen. Any moment now he would return to the pool, fully dressed with a smug smirk on his face. How did he do it? Pulling off a hoax like this surpassed any of Houdini's tricks and illusions.

But he did not return. By now, other teachers and the principal responded to the commotion and were at the poolside. 911 was called and paramedics arrived.

The other boys got dressed and searched the immediate area. Soon they were joined by others as the search expanded.

The pool was emptied and the drain examined and disassembled. Ken's parents were notified to see if he were home. They immediately went to the school and were told what happened. They went into shock and were treated by the paramedics.

Word got out to the community and a small army of volunteers searched for Ken. The search expanded for miles beyond the site of Ken's disappearance.

Mr. Eachus and the boys were interviewed by the police. He tried to tell them what Ken had shared with him about falling - falling forever into a dark void. But the words stuck in his throat. They would think he was a madman, and somehow culpable. Perhaps he was. He was so certain he had done the right thing. But now he doubted his decision. The world was not what he had always believed - a world governed by scientific principles and rationality. He was wrong. There was no sense to any of it anymore. The world was absurd and a place of madness.

Ken was never found.

A few months after he disappeared, Mr. Eachus committed suicide by jumping off a thirty-story building. He left no suicide note. He did not have to. Everyone knew why.

The years passed. The boys who were with Ken at the pool on the day of the plunge went on with their lives, going their separate ways, doing their separate things. No one ever spoke of what happened. But it was always there, haunting their thoughts - haunting their consciences. Ken had counted on them.

And when they would talk with others who were not there, about business, world events, their children, and then grandchildren, their thoughts were never about those things - not truly. And as they grew old, their faces without warning sometimes locked into rictus smiles, inexplicable - as inexplicable as that day in October decades ago.

That day of the Plunge.

The Cavern

Dr. Terlo had been Ed Cummings' physician for over twenty years and felt he was not only Ed's doctor but his friend. Ed called him "Doc," which sounded old school and archaic, but the doctor found it endearing.

"There's nothing much wrong with you, Ed. Your vitals and blood work are fine. Turning fifty isn't what it used to be. Being fifty a hundred years ago was getting up there, but now, with reasonably decent genes and a healthy lifestyle, the odds are excellent that you have a lot more life ahead of you. You're just tired, burnt out. Sales is a stressful profession. What you need is some time off - a vacation."

"Thanks, Doc. It's good to know I'm not falling apart. And you're right about fifty. We've got big earners at the company who are pushing seventy. But I would like to take a vacation - two or three weeks at least and get recharged, but I've done my share of travel; I've been to most of the standard tourist spots around the world and some other places more remote and obscure. What I'd like to do is get away and go somewhere not necessarily far but as different as possible from what I've seen. Any suggestions?"

The doctor thought for a moment, then smiled. "Different - really different? Like being in a different world different?" The doctor's smile was a little bit mischievous and a little bit enigmatic.

"Yeah, that's the idea, Doc. What better way to get away from it all than to go to an other worldly place?"

"Have you ever heard of The Ink Well Caverns in South Carolina?"

"Well Yes, I have. I thought they were closed down for safety reasons."

"Only for a while, Ed. They've since been tested and are as stable as any caverns in the world. What caused alarm was a group of people -

about twelve - disappeared and were never found.
Probably overconfident spelunkers who strayed
from the beaten path. You know they still aren't
sure how deep and how wide those caverns are.
Some people think they make the Carlsbad
Caverns in New Mexico seem like a broom closet
in comparison.

But if you stay on the path and listen to the
rangers it should be quite an experience, and a
safe one as well. The caverns are within a national
park and thousands of people visit them every
year. I've heard it's like walking on the moon."

The flight to Columbia, South Carolina was
uneventful. Ed rented a car at the airport and
drove the ninety miles to the caverns. It was early
October and the weather was perfect. It was warm
and the road cut through forested areas where the
trees were ablaze with Autumn.

There was a small town called Ravenville
where Ed had reserved a room for several nights.
He checked in, and the pleasant concierge at the
desk gave him his key. The man brimmed with
old time Southern hospitality and soon he and Ed
were chatting like long lost friends. Henry was the
concierge's name, and he delighted in telling
customers about the various points of interest
within a few miles from the hotel.

"Do you like museums, Ed? We've got a cluster of them - small museums devoted to things you'd never imagine would be exhibited. THE MUSEUM OF ROADKILL TAXIDERMY is a favorite of visitors, as is THE MUSEUM OF SHOT REVENUERS. You'd be amazed, how many revenuers who were sniffin' around other people's business fell into the moonshiners' cross hairs through the years. But don't worry - none of them got stuffed like the roadkill - just snuffed," Henry quipped with a sly country chuckle.

Ed could not help but laugh. He liked Henry, as he tended to like most down to Earth people.

"Tell me Henry - I heard a dozen or so spelunkers got lost in the caverns some time back and were never found. Is that true?"

Henry's jovial mood was broken. He looked around to make sure there were no eavesdroppers, then replied in a low whisper, "That's what they want folks to believe. Those weren't no spelunkers or cave crawlers as I like to call them. They were a group of tourists, folks like you, just average folks taking the tour like a thousand others. The caverns were shut down for a spell and there was a big investigation. But not to see if the caverns were structurally sound. It was a criminal investigation."

"Criminal," replied Ed. "Why was there a criminal investigation?"

"Those caverns are a fascinating place, Ed, but through the years some of the park rangers have had, well, breakdowns. It's 55 degrees down there, every minute of every day. Without artificial lighting, it's completely dark; that's how they got their name - the Ink Well Caverns. It's blind man's dark - you could put a torch an inch from your eyes and not see a thing without those artificial lights. It's not a head healthy environment to be in day after day. Not everyone can take it - not even some of the rangers."

"So those people who disappeared into the darkness were supervised by a ranger?"

"That's right, Ed. When they found him, he claimed he fainted - blacked out. And when he came to, all those folks were gone."

Ed's face reflected the consternation he was feeling. Perhaps a Mediterranean cruise would have been a wiser vacation choice.

"Now, don't you worry none, Ed. That ranger was investigated thoroughly, and he was given the benefit of the doubt, then let go. The state paid a pretty penny to the tourists' families. But there were changes before the caverns' reopened. Just to be on the side of caution, the rangers are vetted like secret service men and go through an intense psychological examination every year."

Ed went up to his room and unpacked. Old Henry was a character. It would be difficult to suppress something like a dozen tourists disappearing in the caverns, such a thing would be bound to leak and the media would be like pigs at the pastry wagon. "TOURISTS SUCKED INTO CAVE VORTEX" might read the headline, real Bermuda Triangle stuff. People love a mystery, and a hint of the sinister or supernatural adds a special allure. Who knows, perhaps no one disappeared, and their story had become folklore simply to generate business or revenue, as Henry might say.

Ed arose bright and early, jumped in the shower, then got dressed. He grabbed a thick jacket remembering that the caverns were perpetually in the mid-fifties.

After a quick breakfast, he jumped in the rental and drove the three miles to the caverns' entrance.

After buying his ticket, he entered a short line of tourists and was placed in a group of twelve. Among the people in his group were three young couples from Europe - two German and one French. They looked like they were students, out for an adventure before returning to school. The rest were an interesting mix: a father about Ed's age with his wife and teenage daughter, a woman in her thirties with a large camera strapped around her neck, and a man in his mid-seventies, for whom the caverns were an item on his bucket list. Then, the park ranger who would be their guide appeared.

"Hello folks. Welcome to one of South Carolina's most fascinating attractions - The Ink Well Caverns. My name is Ranger Bart Curtis, and I will be your guide for what I guarantee will be an experience you'll never forget."

Ed looked at Ranger Curtis. He was tall and somewhat pale and wore glasses with lenses so thick it looked comical. He looked earnest and affable enough, but there was something incongruous about him in the roll of a park ranger. When he spoke, at various intervals his voice would rise in pitch to the point of being shrill. His adam's apple was prominent and bobbed as if it might pop out of his neck, especially when he got excited describing something fascinating about the caverns. There was an overall high strung quality to him and, most unnerving, he would giggle inappropriately after explaining something he felt should be noted by the group.

The group descended, following Ranger Curtis. Ed felt the temperature drop and zipped up his jacket.

It was truly like another world; a separate, subterranean reality hidden beneath the surface of the world that Ed knew. This was a place of cold darkness barricaded against the light of sun.

Ranger Curtis was in his glory, explaining the myriad phenomena surrounding the group. "Now, don't bump your heads on the stalactites, or stumble on the stalagmites. Do any of you folks know how to remember which is which? No one knows?" The question was spoken with good nature at the beginning but ended on that shrill note Ed had noticed earlier. "Well I'll tell you if no one knows," he snapped. Ranger Curtis was clearly exasperated. "Stalactites are rock formations coming from a cave's ceiling. They have to hold *tight* or they will fall. Stalagmites are rock formations that grow upward from the cave's floor. If they keep growing, they *might* reach the ceiling." Ranger Curtis giggled at his own witticism, then abruptly stopped when he saw that the group was not responding to his humor. A brief flash of anger lit his eyes.

The tour continued. Ranger Curtis appeared sullen and was no longer as informative as he was earlier. Ed looked about him. This world was so strange. Earlier, closer to the surface, there were bats sleeping upside down on the caves ceiling. But the farther they descended, the more lifeless the caverns became.

During the tour, the group was instructed to keep on the narrow, winding path on the caverns' floor. Every few yards on either side of the path were lamps which provided light in order to see. Ed remembered Henry's description of the caverns without artificial lighting - "blindman's dark." It was a strange idea to Ed; this entire underground world with all its surreal rock formations and craters; a dead, unseeable world without the lights.

"All right folks, this is the end of the tour - or at least the basic tour. Just follow the path the way we came to get back to the entrance." Ranger Curtis seemed in better sorts now. Perhaps he was glad it was over and was hoping the next group would be more appreciative of his humor. He looked at his watch "You know folks, I'm way ahead of schedule. I guess I didn't yak as much as I normally do. I'm a full forty minutes ahead." Ranger Curtis looked at the group and smiled somewhat mischievously. "The official tour is over but, when time permits as it does now, I'm sanctioned to take you a bit further - and a bit deeper. It's not on the tour book, but about another 500 feet below us is a large room within the caverns where the rock formations resemble furniture: chairs, tables, and a large couch. It's called the Devil's Lounge. Would any of you like to see it?"

Every person in the group responded in the affirmative. Well, thought Ed, I've come this far - may as well get my money's worth.

"Excellent," exclaimed Ranger Curtis. "You'll never forget this. Follow me and watch your step. The path narrows, and you'll need to walk single file."

The path was winding and somewhat steep. As they descended the rock formations appeared to grow stranger, the stalactites and stalagmites crooked and misshapen. The Devil's Lounge - a man cave for Satan in the bowels of hell.

Finally, they were there. It was unbelievable. How could this be a natural phenomenon? The rock chairs, table, and couch looked uncannily real, as if carved by a master craftsman. There was special lighting above, giving the area a sepia, almost scarlet glow. The group stared at the formation, mesmerized.

Ed reached for his camera, along with several

others, but Ranger Curtis interrupted them. "I know this is an incredible photo op but, before you take pictures, I want you to experience something unique." Ed felt a sudden chill.

"Now I'm sure you've all heard that old philosophical saw, 'If a tree falls in the forest and no one hears it, did it truly make a sound?' Let's apply that question here. If a cavern contains fascinating rock formations, but no one can see them, do they truly exist?"

Ed felt a rush of apprehension. Where was he going with this?

"Now earlier, before the tour began, I'm sure you heard or read that no natural light penetrates the caverns. Everything you see around you is only possible because of the artificial lighting. Now what I'm going to do…" Ranger Curtis paused and giggled, ever so briefly, "is turn off all the lights - just for a brief moment - so you can experience total darkness. Now don't move an inch; within seconds you'll be disoriented - and I wouldn't want you to stumble and fall on some jagged rocks - would I?"

Ed's apprehension was turning into dread. He looked at Ranger Curtis. He saw something that looked like a remote in his hand. He pressed a button and the lights dimmed - then went off.

Ed raised his hand and held it inches from his eyes. Nothing. Blind man's darkness. He started to count. One thousand and one, one thousand and two… after thirty seconds Ed heard a woman's voice, "Please Ranger Curtis - turn the lights back on - we've experienced enough." More than a minute had elapsed. More voices. The loud baritone of a man, "Ok - we get the idea - now turn the God damn lights back on!" A shrill giggle pierced the darkness. The entire group began to shout, then wail in a chorus of hysteria. "Please in the name of sweet Jesus, turn on the lights!"

Ranger Curtis responded. "Now calm down, everyone. You're such sour pusses, excitable sour pusses. Take a deep breath. Good. Now remember - it always looks darkest - right before it gets pitch black!"

There was a scream, followed by more screams. The group flailed and panicked. Ed stumbled over someone and fell to the cavern floor. He felt people stepping on him. He began to crawl, hoping somehow he crawled in the right direction. Amidst the cries and screams, he heard it -a shrill, maniacal giggle growing fainter until it disappeared into the void.

He Loves Us So Much

"Oh, no you don't. You're not going anywhere. You're staying put because you love us so much."

She is so adorable. The mock sternness, melting into playful mischief. Oh, so much like her mother.

She sat beside him as he lay upon the cushion. The cushion: it was so comfortable, so warm and seductive.

Her tiny hand was firm and insistent as she pushed against his chest.

"You're just being silly. You are so silly. We love you. We love you so much!"

He looked at her. Were her eyes green or blue? They seemed to change from moment to moment.

She is so adorable, sitting next to him. He could feel the warmth in her thighs. So adorable. She looked like a small replica of her mother with her knees tucked up to her chest and her cute tiny feet curled into balls.

"Sometimes you just exasperate us. Do you know that?"

 She was so adorable when she furrowed her brows in exasperation. He felt giddy; she was so adorable. Oh, how he loved her so much. She is so precious - so absolutely loveable.

What was that? What sound was that? He heard a sound; he was sure of it. It was a fluttering sound. From somewhere in the room.

He turned his head away from her and, in an instant, she was gone.

He sensed a light and looked to his side. There was an embrasure like window.

He looked out the window. He had to twist and crane his neck to see. Where was he?

He sensed he was in a tower with the clouds below. Were those green hills beneath the cracks in the clouds? Was there a stream? They seemed so small, so distant. There was a golden glow as the cracks in the clouds widened, as if an eternal

October bathed the landscape.

There was a gauze around his memory. How did he get here? Who, exactly, was he?

That flutter sound. He turned from the window. She was back. There was something clasped in her tiny hand.

She began to fuss behind his ear with a moist swab. She whispered, "I love to take care of you. We love to take care of you in every way. You are so sweet, and we love you so much."

He closed his eyes. That flutter sound again - louder, more powerful.

He opened his eyes and she was there.

Oh, she was so beautiful. And so powerful. Her eyes, like her daughter's - so large and bright. She tilted her head to one side and placed her hands on her hips in playful exasperation.

He stirred, ever so slightly.

He looked around. Where was this place? He had never noticed before. The walls were porous, as if he were in an immense hive.

He stirred again and attempted to rise.

"I - I should get up and stretch a bit."

They began to giggle, mother and daughter together.

"Oh, look at him. He is so adorable. Now why in the world would you need to get up? We take care of all of your needs."

She looked down upon her daughter. "Sweetheart, don't we take care of all of his needs?"

"Of course, we do, mother. He is so sweet. So sweet and silly. And we love him so much!"

"But - but why am I...?"

The mother bent down and interrupted him.

"Hush," she whispered in his ear. Her breath was a warm balm. "You know how much you love us - and we love you so much."

For an instant, he felt panic - a need to flee from this strange place. He looked about. The pores in the wall seemed to be moving. He saw, or imagined, grotesque creatures, larva-like, wriggling through the openings.

Then, he felt her hand stroke his head. Her tongue, ever so quickly, darted into his ear.

The panic released. The golden glow from outside seemed to rise above and engulf him. He was awash in a pleasant sense of lassitude.

Oh, why did he have such silly concerns? He began to laugh. They all laughed. The room was filled with laughter.

He laughed so hard the velvety sheet that covered him fell away.

His laughter stopped. He looked down and

shuddered. He had no arms or legs.

"Mother - he sees!" They flew to him. They were happy and excited. They hovered over him as they buzzed and fluttered.

He looked at them. Oh, how his heart swelled. They were so adorable as their gossamer wings made melodic sounds.

"It's only for a little while - then they will grow back."

"Oh mother, do they have to grow back? He is so sweet and looks so silly as he is. "

"I'm afraid so, little one. And he will grow wings, like ours - only bigger and stronger. And then he will be the leader of us all."

"Oh, look at him, mother. We made him only half of what he once was, and now he is so sweet. So much sweeter than the others who screamed and then died. He is so sweet and silly. We love him so much. And he loves us so much!"

She stilled her wings and padded over to him. Her feet were so tiny, so precious. She kissed him lightly and whispered, "You're not going anywhere - you love us so much."

He tried to scream, but there was no sound.

He looked at them.

They were so adorable together. Oh, how he loved them.

He loved them so much.

The Riddle of Norman

It was mid-October when Dorian Bellows and his sister Anne were notified of their uncle Norman's death.

Their uncle had been an eccentric and recluse, and he lived in a large Victorian house which he had leased. He died intestate, and Dorian and Anne were his only relatives and, therefore, his only heirs. His savings had been miniscule, but he did have an extensive collection of antiques. Dorian and Anne had decided to take inventory of the collection and sell those items which seemed to have value through an estate sale.

The drive to the house took about three hours

from San Francisco where both of them lived. Anne drove; Dorian preferred to be the passenger so he could enjoy the spectacle of dazzling colors displayed by the autumn trees and foliage. He had always been prone to daydreaming, and his imagination was pleasantly provoked by the golden landscape and the falling leaves, like brittle snowflakes of red and yellow.

Anne was the practical one: the realist. She was more motivated by closing the books on Uncle Norman's estate than any money from the sale of his antiques. This was more an act of obligation than a business trip. The plan was for Dorian and her to stay a few days at Uncle Norman's house to organize the antiques and a few days more to sell them. What could not be sold would be donated to Goodwill.

When they arrived at the house, they were taken aback by the size of the dwelling: a Queen Anne Victorian of over 3,000 square feet, way in excess for just one occupant. The house itself appeared sinister by virtue of its incongruity. It was completely non-conforming, compared to the other houses in the neighborhood, with its asymmetrical facade, bold gables, and spires like lances puncturing the sky.

Dorian and Anne walked up to the steps

leading to the front door and removed a key from the lock box.

When they entered the house, they were startled by how extensive the antique collection was. Exotic quilts and carpets adorned the floors and walls; there was an array of grandfather clocks, standing tall as if keeping vigil over the myriad of furniture, vases, sculptures, and paintings that populated the living room. No item appeared newer than late nineteenth century and, some, like the collection of swords and a pair of suits of armor were clearly medieval. Despite the density of objects and artifacts contained in the house, there was an order and symmetry in their arrangement creating the impression of an extensive museum exhibit.

"Well, where do we get started, Dorian? Neither of us are antiques experts. Some of these items might have great value, others might be junk. I say we call in an appraiser to get some idea of what we have."

"Yes, yes," he replied. "We should get an expert opinion. But not quite yet. Let's just, well, take a little time to take all of this in. Do you have any memory of Uncle Norman? Mom and Dad rarely mentioned him, rest their souls. I still can't believe they're gone. If they had left for the party a minute earlier or a minute later, they never would have crossed paths with that drunk. Fate."

"There is no fate, Dorian. It was random, just like everything else. And yes, I have a very faint memory of Uncle Norman. I was six and you were an infant. It was a Christmas gathering. All I remember of him was that he was tall and slender and looked completely out of place. The other adults kept their distance from him - almost as if for some reason they were afraid of him."

Dorian surveyed the vast variety of items that seemed to engulf his sister and him. How did Uncle Norman acquire it all? He was not wealthy.

"Let's do a quick rundown of what's here. All of the things we see here might be the tip of the iceberg. This house has three floors plus a basement and attic. Let's start on top and work our way down. We need at least a general idea of the total inventory before contacting any antiques appraiser."

The two of them walked up the steep steps of the stairs. Dorian pondered why Victorian houses always seemed to have unusually high steps. If anything, people were shorter in the nineteenth century, and the steps should be shorter than today's.

When they reached the third floor, they

discovered a separate stairway with even steeper steps leading to the attic. They needed to hold the railing in order to pull themselves to the top. There, they found a thick, oaken door, which required a sharp shove to open.

Surprisingly, the attic was light inside due to a large skylight. Dorian and Anne perused what lay before them.

Against all walls were several cabinets with glass doors. Within the cabinets were medicine bottles of various sizes, shapes, and colors. A closer look showed that the bottles still contained various fluids, potions, and elixirs, in spite of the bottles' obvious age.

In the center of the room was a plain wooden table, conspicuous in its austerity. At the center of the table was a large box covered in black velvet. At the base of the box was a note with these words:

> *Whoever may discover this box,*
> *treat its contents with respect*
> *and caution.*

Dorian looked at Anne. She had seen this look - this expression before. She had seen it when they were children. Whenever Dorian encountered something strange or mysterious, his imagination would reflexively run rampant. Everything that was even slightly enigmatic would be magnified and infused with duplicity. He saw riddles where none existed.

"Well, I'm feeling both respectful and cautious. Let's pull off the veil and see what's inside."

"I have a better idea," replied Anne. "Let's leave it as it is and let the appraiser do the unveiling."

"But why? I want to know now. Such a strange note. So peculiar. What does it really mean?"

"Probably nothing more than it says. Whatever is in the box may be fragile and Uncle Norman wanted it to be handled with care."

"Then why not just 'handle with care,' Anne? That would be explicit and to the point. 'Fragile, handle with care,' is the standard, almost universal identification for something breakable."

"Look, Dorian, you have no memory of Uncle Norman. I do. Young children have an unfiltered perception of people. The other adults kept their distance. There must have been a reason. The more I think of him, the creepier he becomes in my memory. Small details are coming back. I remember that I shuddered when he smiled at me, and I turned my head and walked closer to our parents. Just leave the box alone. Let's go down to the third floor. I'm sure you will find something there of equal fascination."

"This is funny. Ironic in a way. I'm usually the one accused of fantasizing and letting my imagination get away from me. This time it's you. You're behaving as if the box may be booby trapped."

Anne was not sure herself why she was resisting. Perhaps Dorian was right.

"Alright, Dorian. But I'm stepping back a few paces - just in case."

Dorian approached the box. Moving dramatically like a magician about to expose an illusion, he yanked the veil from the box.

He looked at the contents before he carefully removed the items and placed them gently on the table.

There were two books, both of which were quite old and bound in leather: one was Homer's *The Odyssey*, the other the *Grimm's Brothers Fairytales*. The third item was a brass kaleidoscope. The fourth item was an ornate jeweled hand mirror. the fifth item was an old postcard featuring a picture of a calypso dancer. And the sixth was a birthday card circa late 19th century for a nine year old girl.

Dorian stared at the items at length.

"When you've stopped gawking, look at me Dorian. Tell me that you're disappointed with what was in the box. Tell me you wanted something magical and mysterious instead of some miscellaneous junk from a garage sale."

"Don't jump to conclusions, Anne. It might be worth pondering before we move on. Remember the old Zen principle that beneath the ordinary lies the extraordinary? If it's just random items tossed into a box, why the odd note?"

"Because Uncle Norman was an odd man. A very odd man."

"Alright Anne. Humor me. Just humor me for a bit before we move on. What do we know of Uncle Norman? Did mom or dad ever talk about him?"

Memories were surfacing for Anne. Unpleasant memories.

"He was our mother's brother. Her younger brother. He was seldom mentioned, and when he was it was in hushed tones. As I mentioned before, I remember seeing him only once when I was six. Memories. Sometimes memories are better left forgotten."

"Well, what else do you remember? I promise Anne, just give me a bit more about Uncle

Norman. Maybe you're right. Maybe it's just a random hodgepodge of things he tossed in the box and the note is a red herring to incite the imagination of someone like me. You know, I get the feeling you know more, but you're repressing it."

"I have been repressing it successfully until he died and we came to this horrible house. I remember Mom talking to Aunt Nell about Uncle Norman having to go away when he was quite young. I don't think even they knew why. I remember hearing that no one knew where he went. It was like he disappeared for a long time; I think it was ten years. Then, like magic, he was back."

"I wonder if he went on a trek and during that time, he acquired all of these antiques." Dorian looked at the books on the table. "He went on a kind of - well - an odyssey." Dorian suddenly had an inspired look on his face. He picked up one of the books – *The Odyssey*.

"Ok, *The Odyssey* is about the ten years of Odysseus' wandering at sea, trying to return home after the Trojan war. Where did mom and Uncle Norman grow up?"

"In Ithaca, New York - you should at least know that. When our parents married, they moved to California."

"Ah ha! *The Odyssey* is about Odysseus trying to return home after wandering for ten years - home to the island where he was king - the island of Ithaca. Uncle Norman was off on his own odyssey for ten years - then returned home to Ithaca."

Anne looked at Dorian with incredulity - as if he were a lunatic. "You're joking - please tell me you're joking."

"Remember what Carl Jung said - there are no coincidences."

Dorian perused the other items on the table. He picked up the postcard with the calypso dancer. It pictured a lithe black woman in colorful Caribbean garb. As he stared at the image, he could almost see her sensual undulations. Then, he turned back to *The Odyssey*. There was a bookmark extending out from the center.

He opened the book to where it was marked.

"Anne, look. Look where it's marked. Book five - the book that deals with Odysseus being held captive by the sorceress Calypso!"

Anne needed to sit down. She did not know whether to laugh or cry. "Please Dorian. Please tell me you're joking. The fact that Lincoln was assassinated by a Southerner and Kennedy was in a Lincoln when he was shot by a Southerner is a dumb stretch of coincidence just like your Calypso connection. What else? Let's get this out of your system. What meaning can you come up with for the kaleidoscope?"

Dorian lifted the kaleidoscope. Its brass exterior shined beneath the skylight, polished and heavy in his hands, heavier, he thought, than a kaleidoscope should be. He put his eye to the lens and twisted the end of the scope.

The shapes and colors were phantasmagoric. With each rotation, new shapes and colors would appear. Then, he noticed something. It was subtle and almost subliminal at first; he thought it was a flaw in the lens, so he reversed the rotation and saw it again. It was a letter. More slowly now, he rotated the lens and saw another letter.

Through trial and error, he discovered that with every fifth rotation a new letter would appear.

Setting the kaleidoscope down, he asked for and received from Anne a pad and pen to write the letters down after each fifth turn of the lens.

Arual llams.

"Keep me honest, Anne. Look through the scope and turn it slowly. Every fifth turn will show a letter. Read them to me."

Trying to conceal her exasperation, she did as instructed and confirmed the letters.

"And what of it, Dorian? It could be some manufacturing code that wasn't removed during production. You really do see a double meaning in everything. It's crazy."

"Let's not be hasty, Anne. I can almost see something in those letters - something more than randomness."

His eyes suddenly focused on the mirror. Picking it up, he held it to the letters. Then, he reversed the letters.

Laura Small.

Anne gasped. She did not want any of this. Coincidence no longer seemed reasonable. Hidden meanings had always upset her. There was something sinister about them, like predators concealing themselves behind the bushes, eager to strike when revealed.

Dorian next picked up the birthday card. It pictured a child, a pretty little blonde girl with pigtails, carefree and innocent, walking through the woods with a basket in her hand. He opened the card. It said, "Happy ninth birthday to a sweet, pretty little girl." There were no names indicating the recipient or the bearer of the card.

"Anne, does the picture of the little girl

remind you of something - or someone?"

Anne made a decision. She decided to let this fixation of Dorian's play itself out. There was only one item left: the book of *Grimm's Fairy Tales*. After examining the book, he would try to tie everything together.

"Well, it reminds me of some of the fairytales everyone is exposed to as children."

Dorian picked up the book of *Grimm's Fairy Tales*. He smiled as if a smoking gun was about to be discovered. Leafing through the stories, he abruptly stopped. There was something odd used as a book -mark. It was a lock of blonde hair. The lock was within the story of *Little Red Riding Hood*. It was tucked away in the third page from the story's end. And there was something else. Dorian handed the open book to Anne.

She first saw the lock, then her eyes traveled down the page. One line was highlighted. It was the line that terrified her as a child.

"The better to eat you, my dear"

Anne trembled. She handed the book back to her brother and sat down. Her eyes were wide with astonishment.

"Oh Dorian. This has turned into a nightmare. I've buried so much - repressed so much about Uncle Norman. And now those dread memories are rising to the surface.

That day, at the Christmas gathering. Before Uncle Norman smiled at me, he spoke to me. Those words."

"What - what did he say, Anne?"

"He told me he felt like the big bad wolf around me - that he could just eat me up."

Dorian sat down beside his sister. His mood had also changed. At first the treasure hunt - the riddle of Uncle Norman was fun and amusing. Now Anne's nightmare awakening had cast a pall upon him and the riddle.

"Anne, how did you learn of Uncle Norman's death? I learned of it from you - but how did you find out?"

"He died without a will, Dorian. Intestate is the legal term. So Uncle Norman's estate was handled by the county administrator. I received a letter informing me that you and I are the only traceable heirs. I was also informed about the location of his house, and that all of his belongings now belong to us."

"You wouldn't have that letter with you, by chance?"

"No - but I remember the name of the deputy administrator who signed the letter. It was Chase - Arthur Chase."

Dorian sat in silence for a moment, then turned to Anne.

"I have an idea. This can of worms I've opened has given rise to questions that I think can be answered.

All of this - the riddle, this house, the items from the box - have unnerved you. I want you to check into a hotel for a couple of days while I do some research. I have an old college friend named Steve Burton who is a county archivist. He has access to public records, newspaper articles, obituaries - pretty much anything that was recorded or reported going back over a hundred years. Research that might take me a few months he can do in a day or so. Let's uncover the riddle of Norman - who he really was, the lost ten years, what did he die of, and what did he do. Then we can better understand what the items from the box mean. In the meantime, I want you out of here. Let's find a decent hotel where you can stay for a few days. We will stay in touch - I'll call and text you and tell you what I've learned."

Dorian went with Anne as she checked into a small but quality hotel a few miles from Uncle Norman's house. They both agreed that driving back to San Francisco then returning would be too exhausting, especially with Anne's frayed nerves.

Dorian contacted the archivist, Steve Burton. Having Steve as a friend was fortuitous; he was good at his job and enjoyed the research challenges when presented to him.

When Steve heard his old friend's voice he was delighted. He and Dorian were similar in many ways, but Steve was more focused and methodical, especially with research. Where Dorian would try to intuit answers and solutions, Steve was a strict empiricist.

"Dorian - it's good to hear your voice again. How long has it been? Over a year?"

"Just about, Steve. I'm sorry I haven't been very good at keeping in touch and, now, out of the blue, I have a big favor to ask. A research favor."

"Anything for an old friend. On top of that I'm a public servant and research is my thing."

"Thanks Steve. Here's the situation. My sister Anne and I have inherited a number of antiques from an uncle who has passed away. His name is Norman Hunt. While going through some of his property, some questions - disturbing questions - have arisen. Anne was notified of Norman's death by a county administrator named Arthur Chase. Norman had never drawn up a will. We'd like to know how Norman died and his age. We'd also like to know how Arthur Chase got Norman's case.

Our uncle Norman was a bit of a mystery man. He disappeared for ten years, probably about fifty years ago. Where was he? And part of this riddle involves a girl named Laura Small. She may have been nine, and my gut tells me she may connect to Norman's disappearance."

"Can you tell me a bit more about Norman, Dorian? What did he do for a living? Was he ever married? Apparently he had no children, if you and Anne are the only heirs. Are there pictures of him?"

"I was too young to have any recollection of him, but Anne remembers him at a holiday gathering when she was about six. She described him as being tall and slender - and creepy. She remembers him telling her she made him feel like the big bad wolf and that he could eat her up, or words to that effect.

I won't go into every detail, but he left six items in a box with a cryptic note attached. The objects appear to be interconnected clues to a riddle."

"All right, Dorian. Norman Hunt, Laura Small, Arthur Chase, a ten year disappearance of dear old Uncle Norman about fifty years ago. You know Dorian, I've been an archivist for over ten years now, and sometimes I feel that everything that's ever happened has been recorded or memorialized in some way. Even before the internet there was a 'cloud' of information, much of which has been scanned. It's all there, dormant, waiting to be discovered. If what you want to know is knowable, I'll find it; it shouldn't take more than a day - two at the most."

"I'm beholden to you, Steve."

"Yes, you are, Dorian. I'm still a Chivas man. I'll call you when I've got the answers."

Steve Burton in many ways was born to be an archivist. The stereotype of the archivist was of a reclusive introvert cloistered away in a musty basement office, chronicling and filing insignificant and arcane documents. But Steve's approach was far more akin to that of a private detective. He had an intuitive sense of where to look for information - clues - that eventually stitched together into salient facts, and then to logical conclusions. Deeds, maps, property records, marriage notices and obituaries were at his fingertips, but he could also go beyond the public record. He was a risk taker and had learned how to tap into information not meant for public perusal. If ever caught, he would be terminated, but he pushed the envelope when needed and could access private or even confidential information - such as individual medical records and criminal histories. This was one of these times in which he would push beyond prescribed boundaries. He took his job seriously, just as he did friendship.

Dorian had decided to stay at Uncle Norman's house until he received the report from Steve. He had left the car with Anne at the hotel and taken an Uber back to the house. As he waited, he tried to check out the rest of the house and Uncle Norman's myriad antique collection, but he kept getting drawn back to the attic and the enigmatic objects from the box. He would stare at them, nearly transfixed. The blond lock of hair used as a bookmark haunted him most. Where was it from and what did it mean?

Two days had passed. He was growing restless when his mobile phone rang. It was Steve.

"Ok Dorian - are you sitting down?"

"Yes, I am Steve, on an antique Louis XIV chair. What have you got? Spill."

"Here it is: Norman Hunt, born October 14th, 1954, in Ithaca, New York. Parents, Robert and Mary Hunt. From an early age he exhibited sociopathic behavior in the form of torturing small animals and pulling pranks on younger schoolmates, often resulting in injury. Psychiatric treatment began at age ten.

When he was sixteen, he raped and sodomized an eleven-year-old girl and was incarcerated in a psychiatric hospital for the criminally insane located in Calypso, New Jersey. Because he was a minor and the psychiatrists felt he had responded positively to treatment, he was released after ten years at the age of twenty-six.

He appeared to have mainstreamed and entered the antique import business where he thrived.

Are you still sitting, Dorian? Four years after his release, he was the prime suspect in the rape and mutilation murder of a nine-year-old girl named... Laura Small. Portions of her body were eaten, and her killer had taken a lock of her blond hair as a keepsake. The D.A. was chomping on the bit, but there just wasn't enough evidence to charge Norman."

"Steve - one of the items from the box included a blond lock of hair."

There was silence at Steve's end.

"One final discovery Dorian. There is no county administrator named Arthur Chase - and there is no certificate of death recorded for Norman.

Here's what I want you to do. Contact Anne and have her meet you at Norman's house. Put the items back in the box - especially the lock of hair. Then both of you leave - with the box. Drive back to San Francisco - to my office. I've put together all the background data. Then we contact the police. They will want to reopen the Laura Small case."

Anne was in the hotel bar when she received the text: *Anne - meet me back at Uncle Norman's house - ASAP. I'll be in the attic. The riddle is solved. You won't believe your eyes! – Dorian.*

It only took twenty minutes to drive from the hotel to Uncle Norman's house. The repression was loosening its grip, and Anne began to remember other things that long lay dormant. She remembered the heated argument between her parents and how it frightened her as her parents never argued except this one time. She remembered her mother trying to convince her father that it was the proper thing to do, to invite Uncle Norman to the family holiday get together, that he was changed now, and that blood was thicker than water.

She remembered her father swearing, telling her mother that Norman had no human blood flowing in his veins and that he should have been strangled in the cradle. And she remembered when Uncle Norman spoke to her there was a sickening sweet scent coming from him. It was his cologne. It smelled, she thought, like the perfume used by morticians to mask the stench of death and decay.

Anne parked the car in the driveway and walked to the front door. It was unlocked, and she went inside. "Dorian - I'm here. It's Anne," she called from the parlor. He probably cannot hear, she thought, if he was in the attic.

She began walking up the stairs, which now seemed endless. She had to pause to catch her breath, then continued until she came to the attic door. "Dorian - it's Anne. I'm here." There was no answer. She pushed on the door, expecting resistance, but there was none. She stepped inside. Where was Dorian?

She walked to the table where the box had been, but it was gone. Only one of the items from the box remained. It was the birthday card for the nine year old. "Dorian, this isn't funny. I mean it. Come out from hiding." There was silence. Her eyes were wide, and her hands trembled.

She picked up the card. Something looked different. She looked closer. Everything was the same - a little girl with pigtails, walking and carrying a basket, but - she looked closer. One of the little girl's pigtails was missing, and the little girl's face was changed. It was her own face from when she was a child.

She opened the card. As she did a sickening sweet odor was released. There was a note inside.

Her breath came in rasps and a dizzy nausea curdled from within as she read:

"Dear Anne, my sweet, desirable child,
so innocent and vulnerable.
All these years, I've kept you in my heart.
Such a pretty little
girl, all grown up now. Dorian had to go
away, but I
am here to keep you company. Now turn
around,
sweetheart, and give Uncle Norman a
hug."

That Silver Tongued Devil

"All I can say is that Mr. Mack is one silver tongued devil."

Jane Dowell was the owner and proprietress of the boarding house where every night she would hold court with her boarders. They were like family to her.

The most recent among them was Tom Neal, who moved in three months ago. He was a strong earnest young man of twenty-five who worked in the town's foundry. The senior resident was Issobel Beecher, the forty something town's librarian. She moved in ten years ago and was a perfect fit for Jane's boarding house. She was quiet, befitting her profession, and very polite. In the middle were Harry Stone, a clerk at the dry goods store and just south of fifty and, Priscilla Harper, a pretty seamstress in her early thirties who was a bit high strung but enjoyed the occasional off color joke.

"Well, Miss Jane," commented Harry, "I've heard tell Mr. Mack could convince the devil himself to move to the North Pole."

"That's right," added Tom. "I haven't lived in Fairville as long as you folks but, almost as soon as I set foot here, I overheard people chatting about Mr. Mack; people commenting on his book learnin' and huge vocabulary. Persuasive - that's what they said about him, that he had the power of persuasion."

"I've only seen him twice," stated Issobel. "Such a tall, distinguished looking gentleman. I've been told that he keeps to himself a great deal, that his own collection of books is so vast that he seldom needs to come to the library. I'll never forget the title of the book he checked out; it was the most obscure book in the entire collection. It was only checked out once - only by Mr. Mack."

"Well pray tell," injected Priscilla. "What was the title of the book?"

"I'll never forget, Priscilla. It was titled, *Burial*

Techniques Of The Ancient Celtic People."

"Tarnation," said Jane. "Only a highly educated man like Mr. Mack would be interested in such a book. A real scholar that man is."

"I've heard tell that Mr. Mack is a retired attorney from a big eastern city. Now those fellas know how to persuade," said Harry.

"I heard different," said Tom. "I heard he's from back east, like you heard, but the word I got was he was a professor at one of those fancy ivy league schools."

"I would not be surprised one bit," stated Issobel, "if he was both. A professor of law at a highly respected university like Yale or Princeton. Oh, such a tall, distinguished man, and…" she paused and blushed. "And handsome. And such bearing. The bearing of an important, influential man."

Harry's face lit up. "That's the best word for him, Issobel - influential. He has the power to influence other people and persuade them to do the reasonable thing."

Issobel responded to Harry's observation. She spoke, barely above a whisper. "If I dare to share something with all of you, will you promise to never tell another soul?"

"Yes, yes," they all chimed collectively.

"Of course, we'll never tell anyone," added Priscilla. "Let's all of us hold hands and swear an oath." They all grasped hands. "Jane," continued Priscilla, "You are the owner of our wonderful home, and our leader." A bit of ingratiation never hurt, she thought, especially with one's landlady. "You slate the oath."

"Here, here," they all heartily conferred.

Jane was truly honored and took a deep breath. "All present at this table are more than my boarders and, yes, even more than friends. We are family. And we swear by our blood that we could never betray our dear Issobel and will take her secret to the grave!" Jane felt a stir of pride, taken aback by her own eloquence.

Issobel held tight to the hands beside her. "When Mr. Mack returned the book, he and I were the only ones in the library. He approached my desk and placed my hand in his. His hands are so large and powerful for a gentleman, but his grasp was firm and gentle. Then, with his deep and resonant voice he said, 'My dear Issobel, you are the sentinel of knowledge in our quaint and lovely town. Always remember this: to be chaste through ignorance is no virtue; to be seduced by reason is no vice.' Then... then he kissed my hand."

"Oh my god!" declared Priscilla as Issobel

blushed to near scarlet. "Oh, such a suave and sophisticated gentleman."

"Well, tarnation above," added Tom. "That Mr. Mack could charm the rattle off a copperhead."

"And I bet the darned snake would thank him for it!" exclaimed Harry.

There was quiet for a moment, then Jane spoke. "You know, we've all heard the stories about - well, you know, about how Mr. Mack just takes care of matters. With his reason and his eloquence, I mean. I think it's just a marvel how he keeps our little town, well – tranquil."

"There have been some mighty bad apples in this town through the years," responded Harry. "Men you'd think no one could reason with but somehow, Mr. Mack, with his intellect and silver tongue, can."

"You know," said Tom, "Mr. Mack is such a distinguished looking gentleman, sometimes you don't notice what a big man he is. He must be six feet five or so. And, have you ever noticed his hands? They look bigger and stronger than the mitts on ole' Hank the blacksmith."

"Oh, I wish I could have been a fly on the wall when he reasoned that thief Bart Tooley out of town. Can you imagine - stealing money right out of the church basket on the one Sunday when everyone managed to tithe? Mr. Mack seduced him with reason, and lickity split Tooley was gone. Last October it was," remembered Harry.

"Funny, ain't it," said Tom. "The prior October he reasoned Deke Hartly away too - and good riddance it was, after beating up poor Mr. James. A frail old man who never hurt nobody don't deserve no beating no how."

"If you ask me," opined Jane, "Mr. Mack's persuasive reasoning prowess was at its peak when he convinced Ralph Tiller to high tail out of town. Oh, I hope all them stories about Ralph and little children ain't true. But just in case, Mr. Mack paid him a visit for a reasoning session and next day he was gone! Mr. Mack's purity of persuasion and logic was so - what's the word? - compelling; that's it, compelling - that Ralph left all his belongings and bank account behind."

"Oh, if only I could have been there to observe and listen," added Issobel, face still a flush and eyelashes still a twittering. "I can visualize Mr. Mack, so tall and distinguished, stepping up to that dreadful Ralph Tiller like Cicero stepping up to a podium before the Roman senate explaining calmly and without passion or rancor, with precise logic and clear reasoning that it would be best for all - for the greater good of the community - to simply go away."

"I think Mr. Mack may have missed his calling," expressed Harry. "He would have been a wonderful preacher, guiding folks away from their sinful ways and joining ranks with the righteous. He'd combine faith with reason and would guide folks gently, with his persuasion - and hands that could squeeze the juice out of a coconut."

"I wonder," mused Priscilla, "if he ever married? Mr. Mack, so distinguished and handsome, with his eloquent silver tongue and all. I would imagine the young ladies would be drawn to him like iron to a magnet - a powerful, virile magnet."

"Oh Priscilla!" exclaimed Issobel. "You mustn't talk that way about such a distinguished gentleman like Mr. Mack!"

"Well," declared Jane, with a conspiratorial tone, "I know that Mr. Mack was married - for a spell. Folks don't like to talk about it, what with Mr. Mack being such a distinguished gentleman and all. And I hear tell she was a real harpy!"

"Oh, how terrible," exclaimed Issobel. "Mr. Mack deserved more. His wife should have been refined and educated like her husband. What happened to her?"

"Well," continued Jane, "one day he and his wife sat themselves down and had a long talk. And Mr. Mack, plying his reason and persuasion, along with compelling logic, convinced her that they should divorce and that she should go back to Boston where her rich folks lived, and that's what she did."

"Oh, poor Mr. Mack," observed Priscilla.

"And the very next day," continued Jane, "she was off to Boston, never to return. But there was a silver lining for Mr. Mack. His ex-wife was a woman of means and, because she was so cruel to Mr. Mack, he wound up with her fortune in the settlement. That's why today he is a scholarly man of leisure."

There was an abrupt interruption in their conversation. Fred Rawlings, the town's head clerk, burst into Jane's dining room.

"Sorry to interrupt your supper, folks. One of our neighbors has - disappeared. Isaac Bryer, the new sixth grade schoolteacher, has gone missing. Any of you know where he might be?"

Jane and her boarders looked upon one another, nonplussed. "Why, no Fred," answered Jane. "Where - where might he be?"

"Well," Fred replied, "there was a problem at

the school in Mr. Bryer's class." Fred was a bit winded then caught his breath.

"Well, Isaac - Mr. Bryer - is evidently quite a religious fellow. One of the boys in his class - Nathan Ferris - apparently used our Lord's name in vain."

"No - no Fred," said Jane. "I know that boy. He does chores for the older folks, asking for nothing in return. He's a good boy."

"Well, the report is, Nathan used the Lord's name in vain when he bumped his knee really hard on his desk, and Mr. Bryer washed his mouth with soap in front of the entire class - not once, but several times. And Nathan got sick - real sick."

"What happened next?" asked Jane.

"Well, Nathan got taken to Doc Norton. It was bad for a time, but he's ok now."

"Well - what happened to Mr. Bryer?"

"The school nurse, Miss Deaver, thought Mr. Bryer needed a good talking to. Mr. Shaw, the school principal, is somewhat of a timid soul with a tendency to stutter. So she told Mr. Mack, who everyone knows is an expert at reasoning with folks."

They all looked at Fred with bursting curiosity.

"Well, Mr. Mack took Isaac aside in private

and talked to him. We all know how Mr. Mack can reason and persuade."

Jane and her boarders looked at one another. Issobel began to blush at her private thoughts. Oh, she mused, it must be wonderful - perhaps even blissful - to be seduced by reason by Mr. Mack. Oh, to swoon in rapture and be swept off her feet by persuasive logic. Then, she was shaken from her reverie by the voice of Harry Stone.

"That silver tongued devil, Mr. Mack. Looks like we'll be recruiting a new sixth grade teacher."

Searching for Teddy

He awoke and wondered if there was reason enough to get up.

How did it come to this? When he was young, he never thought he would be old. Not because he was deluded by the myth of youth's invincibility - no, it was because he had been deathly ill as a child, and he would be gone before the flame of youth flickered out. But he was wrong.

He had become a recluse. How did it come to this? Had he not been decent and compassionate to others? His friends had not died, but the friendships had.

When he retired, he hoped new horizons -

new friends would fill the void and the vacant hours, but it was not to be. He felt exiled by circumstance and the blur of time as the days and months vanished from the calendar.

Every morning it seemed to take a little longer to get out of bed. He would make lists of things to do; plans to break out of the doldrums. But lethargy and chronic pain were constant obstacles. Then, the afternoon drowsiness set in.

Sometimes, in the middle of reading a book or watching TV, he would nod off only to be awakened by the whip snap of his neck; at times, the book would fall out of his hands as wakefulness slid away from him.

He began taking naps on his couch. Sometimes, he sensed the cushions were pulling him downward. The sensation was like an unwelcome seduction. The naps became more frequent and of greater duration.

Then, one day in October, he awoke from a nap. He was disassociated. For a horrible moment, he did not know where he was or who he was.

Was this one manifestation of death? Not sudden or violent, but slow and insidious - a seductive disintegration, the will and the senses smothered by a relentless veil of sleep?

Not yet. He fought and clarity returned. He

rallied his will and shook off the malaise and went out for a walk. Just steps from his door, he saw the notice on the lamppost:

Missing Dog
Teddy
Service dog with special needs

He called the number on the notice.

A man answered and explained that the cleaning woman left their door open and Teddy bolted out. He and his wife were frantic and despairing. Teddy was a house dog requiring a special diet; his chances of surviving out on the street were poor.

He began to search. He kept a picture of Teddy with him. The black poodle with gentle eyes; the service dog. Could he have gotten far?

Each day, he arose early, walking the streets and parks near Teddy's home. He made frequent stops to rest. He checked the local animal hospitals and shelters daily. He would ask passersby if they had seen a dog like Teddy. No one had.

On the third week of his search, while walking uphill, he felt a choking sensation, then collapsed.

He woke up in the hospital. He had suffered a stroke, affecting the left side of his body. He was placed on blood thinners and prescribed physical therapy. He did not have time. Teddy was out there. He knew. Teddy was lost and he would find him.

Two weeks later, his search resumed. Once, around a corner within a cluster of bushes, he saw Teddy - he was certain of it. He tried to run toward him - the sweet innocent dog who had lost his way.

He lost his balance and fell on the hard pavement. He got up and struggled toward the bushes where he would find Teddy, frightened and alone. When he got there, Teddy was gone.

Months went by. He limped now, and the left side of his face drooped. The notices of the lost dog had been taken down and he lost the phone number. He carried a cane and looked in small nooks and obscure corners. People gawked. He did not care if they thought he was a fool or a madman. His eyes were wide with the madness of conviction.

A million to one? It did not matter. He knew. Teddy was out there. He would find him. If he did not, no one else would.

The Absurdity

It was mid-October, and Nick and Jeremy were on their way to do a job.

They drove in a not quite vintage yet Ford convertible, top down. Why not? It still felt like summer.

Jesus, Nick reflected. How long had the two of them been doing this?

They met in college over forty years ago. Nick was a philosophy major, and Jeremy majored in English lit. Jeremy met Nick between classes; he literally stumbled over his legs as Nick lay supine beneath a tree, smoking a joint. Nick apologized to Jeremy and offered to share his joint. Their friendship began, right then and there.

There was nothing in their background that portended what they would become. Both of them sold a little weed to make ends meet when they were in school. After graduating they continued to sell; it was more lucrative than the salaries they pulled in from their legal occupations. Then, they partnered when cocaine got big.

Now they were making some real money. It was not so much greed that drove them or the allure of excitement and danger. They both saw things the same way. They would often look at one another and, without a word, start laughing. It was the absurdity of it all. A couple of humanities majors who were not very tough or street wise, who were actually somewhat risk aversive - were becoming substantial players in the cocaine trade.

Then the turning point.

They were to meet a trio of buyers from France who wanted twelve kilos of quality cocaine. The greater the gain the higher the risk. An old timer in the trade who had taken them under his wing told them for stakes that high, never to meet the buyers alone. What he meant was, bring some heat, concealed. He gave them four handguns, two for each of them, and gave them a crash course tutorial. Neither Nick nor

Jeremy had ever fired a handgun before.

They met the Frenchmen out in the desert, a few miles from Bishop. It was January, and cold. They wore thick jackets; the better to conceal their guns.

They pulled their van up beside the Frenchmen's jeep and stepped out. Nick and Jeremy decided during shooting practice that if a rip off looked imminent, to shout "**NOW!**" and start shooting.

Two of the Frenchmen were large, cold looking, and swarthy. The third, the spokesman, was slender, almost androgynous in appearance.

"Do you speak French, gentlemen?" the spokesman queried.

"Not a word," replied Nick. It was a lie. He spoke and understood French quite well, as his grandmother was French Canadian and spoke only French around Nick as he grew up.

The spokesman turned to his comrades and said in French, "Wait until I open the sack and check the bricks then, when I close the sack, kill them."

Jeremy dropped the sack at the Frenchman's feet. As soon as he bent over to open the sack, Nick screamed "**NOW!**"

They both got the drop on the Frenchmen.

There was no hesitation. They drew and fired, a split second before the Frenchmen.

Then there was quiet. All three Frenchmen lay dead. Neither Nick nor Jeremy were hit. Nick looked at Jeremy. He was calm, but there was a faint flush on his face.

They retrieved the money and the cocaine, then drove away from the desert. A few miles back on the freeway, they looked at each other and laughed. It was the absurdity of it all.

Word got out about the two college kids who really knew how to kill; soon their drug days were over, and they entered their true calling - contract hit men. It was absurd.

Their longevity in their new profession was as remarkable as the longevity of their partnership. Forty years is a long stretch by any standard. They never saw each other outside work. They now both had wives, children, and grandchildren. Both told their wives they were commodity salesmen, without providing further details of the nature of the commodities. Incredibly, their wives never displayed any curiosity. And now they were en route to the suburbs of San Diego for another assignment.

They were driving through the desert with no other cars behind or ahead for miles. After passing a truck stop, a motorcycle appeared at their rear. The biker was moving up on them fast and the road had become one lane.

The biker wanted to pass, so Nick, who was at the wheel, slowed down.

The biker sped up, but miscalculated the turn and spun out. The motorcycle skidded, then went down.

Nick backed up to see if the biker was hurt. He wasn't, but he was furious.

He stood up, brushed the dust off his leather jacket, and removed his helmet. He had long red hair, a goatee, and looked about twenty.

"You OK, son?" asked Nick. The biker was seething. "No I'm not OK, you old fuck. You should have slowed down quicker. Old assholes like you shouldn't be allowed to drive. You're probably half blind and senile. You…"

Before the young man could continue his diatribe, Nick pulled out his Glock and shot him between the eyes. Then he floored the gas pedal. Jeremy looked behind as the biker became a small dot, then disappeared beneath the horizon. "Why did you do that?" asked Jeremy.

"He was a menace to society with his recklessness, with the added authority of being disrespectful to his elders. He needed - well, he needed to be disciplined."

"Disciplined?" replied Jeremy. "Doesn't discipline suggest a painful lesson administered on the disciplined in order to correct his future behavior? That punk no longer has a future. What you did, my friend, was draconian."

Nick smiled. Forty years together. He remembered the first contract hit they did as partners. It was near Lancaster and, as they drove back to L.A. Fleetwood Mac was on the radio, they had their first argument. Jeremy insisted that Stevie Nicks was the face and soul of the band. But Nick couldn't see it. Christine McVie was by far the better singer and the true muse for the entire band. He told Jeremy that Stevie couldn't wear Christine's tampon, and Jeremy was offended by the vulgar metaphor. Jesus Christ - they had just splattered the brains of a Columbian cocaine trafficker and his two bodyguards without a flinch, but saying tampon prickled his sensibilities. The two of them had never discussed their respective childhoods. Maybe when Jeremy was a boy he had an earache and his mother told him he couldn't go out to play unless he put a cotton swab in his ear. Maybe he looked for the swabs in the bathroom and found a box of his mother's tampons and figured they were made for earaches, with the little strings on the ends to make them easier to remove. Maybe he stuck one in his ear and went out to play and the other boys, less innocent than Jeremy, knew what they were really for and ridiculed him without mercy. "Hey, look at Jeremy - he really is a pussy," they might have said. Poor Jeremy. Of the two of them, he was the sensitive one. And yet, his sensitivities were easily compartmentalized. Of the two of them he was also the more cold blooded - the better killer.

"You know what they say, Jeremy," stated Nick. "Spare the child and spoil the rod." There. A bit of dyslexic wit should lighten the moment. How could his wordsmith English major partner not appreciate such droll humor? Why, Nick's rod, his shiny Glock, needed exercise or it would gather rust.

Jeremy looked at Nick and they both began to laugh. But the laughter was not inspired so much by the humor. It was the absurdity. The absurdity of who they were and what they had become. The absurdity of life and its tenuousness and how abruptly it can end.

Jeremy looked at his partner. When they began their partnership they both sported ponytails. Now they didn't have enough hair between them to tie and clasp. In some ways being of Medicare age was an advantage. They had fallen off the profile grid, and it gave them a jump on their victims - or targets, as he preferred to think of the people they dispatched. The element of surprise. Most of those targets were men who were armed and aware of their surroundings. When they were confronted by two men who could be their fathers, or even grandfathers, they couldn't believe their eyes until it was too late. It was just in the last few years that Jeremy was prone to reflection. Why did he not think of himself as a monster? He could feel compassion, as he had for the hapless young biker. He had been a loving husband and father, in spite of the lie to his wife regarding his profession. Commodities salesman? It always seemed so ludicrous. He often wondered, of late, if the woman he loved and lived with for over thirty years actually knew what he really did and was either in denial or a state of philosophical acceptance. Long ago he had come to terms with what he and Nick did. It was one of the few times they analyzed their behavior. Both of them reconciled - or perhaps rationalized - that the men they killed (and they had all been men) were violent, just as they were, but their violence was essentially different. They killed indiscriminately, as a means to an end, and many times they killed the innocent either directly or collaterally. Nick and he preyed on the predators. The killing they did made the world a safer place, or so they had convinced themselves. But still, Jeremy thought, how did he get to where he was now? His childhood was stable and normal with no exceptional trauma to set in motion what he would become. Perhaps he became what he was, regardless of externals. He may have been born to be a killer. It was in his blood, in the marrow of his soul - if there was such a thing.

They were almost there. It was October everywhere. The trees on the sides of the road were golden and blood red. Again, the absurdity. They had driven through the gates of a seniors only community. They were assigned Eddie Demarco, the former enforcer for the Polucci family. Why even bother? The man was in his eighties, but he could still talk. Someone wanted to tie up loose ends. It might not be as easy as it appeared. Many of the old guard kept muscle around them.

"You know Nick, let's make this the last one."

"You've been saying that for years," replied Nick.

"No, I mean it this time. I'm supposed to be retired from the commodities business. The grandkids are getting suspicious. They don't believe it anymore when I tell them you and I are out bowling. They think I'm too decrepit to bowl. Maybe it's time."

Nick stared at this old friend - his very old friend. As they got closer to their target's unit, they noticed two large, tough looking young men milling around, observing. They parked, then slowly walked toward the unit. Almost in sync, the young men followed them. They both slowly reached inside their jackets. Nick looked at them through the corner of his eye and nodded to Jeremy.

"**NOW!**" he screamed.

Nick looked at Jeremy and saw the flush of excitement on his face getting brighter as the young men closed in.

Then, he felt like he was falling, drifting backwards, sliding down a hill of memory. He laughed as he fell, then heard Jeremy's laughter blending with his. The absurdity. The absurdity of it all.

It was just like forty years ago. It was just like the first time.

As he fell, he could hear the crackling of

October leaves, and the sweet sound of Christine
McVie's voice.

What Hit Him?

John Morris had just finished work. It was already dark in the declining Midwest town where he grew up and had become a dye maker. He made good money and his job was secure, in spite of the changing times.

It was October and far colder than October should be. As he drove, he looked at himself in the rear view mirror. He was good looking, in a craggy kind of way, early forties; an unmarried loner.

He slowed as he noticed a loose pile of boxes at the side of the road. The broken stack of cardboard was moving.

He pulled over and approached the pile. He could hear sad sounds like those of a hurt animal or whimpering child. Pulling the boxes apart, he was taken aback. There was a girl, no more than a child, in a fetal position and trembling.

John quickly removed his jacket and wrapped it around the girl. "Why are you out here?" he asked. "You'll catch your death of cold."

Her voice came in shivering rasps. "I have no place to go."

John was flummoxed. His small town had no shelters and the girl looked sick. Reluctantly, he picked her up. She was small and light. "Come home with me. I'll give you food and a warm bed until we figure something out."

When they arrived at John's house, he carried his sad little bundle inside and turned up the heat. He took her to an extra bedroom. No one had slept there in years, but he felt a need to keep clean sheets and linens on the bed, just in case. John pulled the covers and gently placed the girl in bed. "Try to relax," he told her. "I'll heat up some soup for you."

He returned with a bowl of chicken noodle soup. She still seemed chilled, so John spoon fed her. She took each small sip like a hungry kitten. She looked so sad and wounded. John was a good man. He wanted to protect her. Soon, she finished her soup and drifted off to sleep.

Before he retired for bed, he noticed her open backpack on the floor. He picked it up and placed it on a chair. Her wallet was open, and he looked at her I.D. Her name was Grace, and she was nineteen. He looked at her in slumber; she looked several years younger. He could not help breathing a sigh of relief that he did not have a minor in his home.

John hit the sack and was asleep within moments; after an hour or so, he awakened with a start. He turned his head and Grace was in bed with him, hugging his back from a fetal position.

"Please don't be mad - I was scared and having a bad dream." She was snuggled tight against him. John got a better look at her. Her large blue eyes were wide with need and innocence. Her hair was dark brown, medium length. She was small, but even beneath the covers he could see curves that swayed with her breathing.

"My name is Grace,' she told John. Her voice was barely above a whisper. "But everyone calls me Gracie."

"My name is John," he replied. Somehow it seemed absurd given the position he was in, but he reached beneath the covers and shook her hand.

"John - no," she said with a wisp of a smile. She corrected him. "No – you're Johnny."

John arose early to go to work. Gracie was still asleep as he stepped into the shower. When he came home from work, he thought he and Gracie would discuss where she could stay - perhaps the neighbors. Fran and Jane Lombard were kind and caring people, and their own kids had left the nest. It would be more proper if Gracie stayed with them until she could get her bearings.

When John returned home from work, he opened the door, then stepped back. Was he in the right house? The air was so clean and fresh. When he walked inside, he saw Gracie. She was wearing bikini panties, one of his shirts which was ridiculously too large on her, and a pair of his socks. She was cleaning, moving with a joyful energy as she worked.

She stopped when she saw John and walked up to him. "Please don't be mad, Johnny. I wanted to make myself useful. I cleaned around and under everything and put everything back exactly in the same spot. I scrubbed everything - every single nook." Gracie stood up on her toes so she could whisper in his ear. "It needed it!" she said, as she crinkled up her nose like a cute bunny.

John could not disagree. His housekeeping was cursory at best. How Gracie could make the house shine in a matter of hours was incredible.

"Thank you, Gracie. Everything looks fresh and clean. You did a wonderful job. You deserve a reward. How about a delivered dinner? What's your favorite kind of food?"

Gracie's face lit up like a child's on Christmas morning. "Chinese, Johnny. I just love Chinese food!" she blurted as she gave John a hug.

John called Shanghai Express, the town's only Chinese restaurant and soon the food was delivered.

Gracie was ravenous and inhaled her kung pau chicken and sweet and sour pork. John noticed she did seem underweight and a bit pale. He wondered how long she had been on the street. She was such a strange young woman. On one level she seemed even younger than nineteen and bore an innocence that suggested surviving homelessness would be tenuous at best. Perhaps when he found her she was only recently without support and a place to stay.

The meal was finished. Now it was time for tea and fortune cookies. Gracie cracked open her cookie: *"Your fortune will suddenly change; trust the fates."*

How could such a message be anything but positive? She shrieked with joy and gave John a quick peck on his forehead.

John cracked open his cookie: *"Relax - you'll never know what hit you."*

"What does it say Johnny?"

"Now is not the time, Gracie." His response was vague and could itself be from a fortune cookie. He quickly stuffed the fortune into his pocket.

"Oh, tell me Johnny - I want to know."

"It's kind of embarrassing, Gracie." It was a small fib. He did not want Gracie to know because the message could be taken as either a bad or good omen. "I'll tell you what, Gracie. When we've gotten to know each other a bit more, I'll share it with you."

Gracie smiled and gave John a hug.

A new pattern had developed. At bedtime they would go to their respective rooms. After John would fall asleep, Gracie would sneak into John's room and get in his bed. The first night, John awoke at two A.M. and found Gracie asleep and snuggled close to him. John was startled when he saw his hand was resting beneath her panties, several inches below the small of her back. Slowly, he removed his hand. The poor girl probably had another bad dream. It was an isolated event, and John went back to sleep.

But a pattern developed. Now, every night when they went to bed, John would pretend to be asleep. Gracie would quietly pad into his room, then get in bed with him. After a few moments, thinking John was asleep, she would place his hand into her panties, now several inches below the small of her back. When John would remove his hand, feigning sleep, he could feel Gracie softly put it back. John decided that in the morning he would discuss this with her.

Gracie would arise a few moments after John and make coffee. He watched her as she moved around in the kitchen. She looked so sweet and childlike.

"Gracie, I think we need to talk about something. I don't know if it's – well, proper for you to come to bed with me every night. I'm a good deal older than you, and…" without saying a word, Gracie walked up to John and gently placed her forefinger to John's lips. It was such a sweet, innocent gesture, and yet there was a firmness to it. John felt an odd, almost giddy vanishing of his resolve, and decided to perhaps bring the matter up later. Then, before leaving for work, he told Gracie she could stay with him for a bit longer, until she got back on her feet. So as not to hurt her feelings, he left the offer open ended.

Another pattern had evolved. When John would return home from work, Gracie would have dinner prepared. He discovered that she was an excellent cook.

The two of them would have dinner together in the evenings, then watch T.V. She was such a quiet girl, but she could communicate volumes through facial expressions and body language. Her sensitivity was extreme. She was especially sensitive to animals. If an animal was being hurt in a movie she would wince and thrust her head against John's shoulder. He learned to screen programs for violence and tried to narrow their viewing to shows with no violence and with happy endings.

It had been three weeks and John felt Gracie should be gently weaned from him.

Before leaving for work, John handed Gracie an envelope.

"Gracie, you have very few clothes, and most are old and worn. Here's three hundred dollars. I'd like you to buy some new clothes, then we can go job hunting."

He expected Gracie to react negatively, as if

she were being pushed out. Instead, her face lit up and she gave John a hug.

John finished work and decided to stop at the local mom and pop store to buy some beer. HANK'S GENERAL STORE AND CAFE was the social hub for the men - "the old timers" as John liked to call them. Most of the community bought their groceries there and everyone knew everyone else.

John walked inside and was immediately greeted by the cantankerous but good natured old timers drinking coffee in the cafe. All of them were leering at him. "You dog," exclaimed Gus, one of the senior old timers. John was taken aback by the statement. "I always knew there was a reason I liked you, John," added Jack. "You dog," continued Gus. "You barking, yelping dog from hell!" The manner in which Gus spoke suggested he was complimenting John rather than insulting him.

"All right," responded John. "What the hell are you guys talking about?"

"Well, John," responded Hank, the store's owner and manager. "There was a young lady here earlier. The cutest, sweetest little thing, quiet but polite and cheerful. Well, she bought up half the store - mostly food and some cleaning items.

She spent close to three hundred dollars. When I introduced myself and asked who she was, she beamed like a new bride. She told me she was your wife."

John was flabbergasted. Was Gracie delusional? He would have a serious discussion with her, tell her to get therapy - to get her head straight, so she could become independent.

John tried to calm himself as he drove into the garage. He took a deep breath then opened the door to the house.

There was an aroma that dumbfounded him. He could not believe his own nostrils.

When John was a child, his mother would cook a very special stew. It contained chicken, sausage, potatoes, carrots, leeks, onions and spices - mysterious spices which John's mother was secretive about, as if she and she alone would know how to apply them. It was slow cooked, simmered, and the aroma would permeate through the entire house. It was absolutely delicious, and if he ate it when he was sad he would become happy. If he was sick it would make him well. And if he was angry it would make him calm. Gracie was cooking his mother's stew! How could it be? When his mother passed several years ago, he assumed she never wrote down the recipe and took the secret with her.

Gracie was tending to the stew in the kitchen - again wearing one of his shirts and a pair of his socks and an apron covering her underwear.

"Gracie - what's happening? I gave you three hundred dollars to buy clothes and you..." Gracie smiled innocently and placed her finger on John's lips, silencing him.

"Please don't be upset, Johnny. A few days ago I was cleaning and tucked behind some papers in a drawer I found your mom's recipe for the stew. I just had to cook it for you."

John felt his resolve weaken, almost to the point of giddiness. "But Gracie" ... he paused as the stew's aroma wafted in the air. "How could you know how to make the stew? My mom was secretive about the spices she used; they're not in the recipe."

She went up on her toes and whispered in his ear, "I just know, Johnny. I just have a sense for what you like and need." John's giddiness increased - he felt as if his knees might buckle.

The two of them sat down to eat. It was surreal - dream like. The stew was exactly like his mother made it. It was delicious beyond description.

Gracie had bought a bottle of merlot which

they drank with their meal. Beneath the table she rested her feet on John's.

"Tell me more about yourself, Gracie. I know so little."

She lowered her head and was silent. She was not ready. Her life, he surmised, was not a pleasant one. Without speaking a word, he knew there was a world of suffering within her. Then, tentatively, she spoke.

"I've been hurt most of my life, Johnny. I've been hurt by men - all over, inside and out. Starting with my own father." Gracie choked back a sob.

John took her hand and held it, gently, as if cradling a small hurt animal.

"It's O.K. honey - you don't need to say more."

She rested her head on his shoulder. "You're a decent man, Johnny," she whispered." I've never known a decent man."

They returned to their meal, and the mood lightened. The wine was heady and good.

When they finished, Gracie took all of the dishes and washed them. John was tired, and his eyelids began to droop.

When Gracie finished the dishes, she sat next to John. He looked so tired. "Johnny - we're both tired. Let's go to bed."

John was so tired he could barely move. Gracie undressed him and helped him to bed; then, for the first time, she undressed and directly got into bed with him.

John awoke at two A.M. He was exhausted. So many years of being alone, of being a creature of habit. Gracie had turned his life upside down. He was conflicted and it was taking a toll on him - and yet?

It was dark, but John could feel Gracie beside him. She was sound asleep. Like nights before, he saw his hand was beneath her panties. This time he left it there. Gracie's hand was resting on his upper thigh.

A new routine began. Gracie would sleep late, and John did not disturb her as he left for work. What was happening to him? He had chanced upon this hapless child; this innocent young woman, so strange and quiet, so filled with sadness that was lifted when she was with him. The original plan was gone. Just a few days, or a few weeks, just enough time for her to reconnect with someone or something positive from her past. But she was so needful - needful for him. And with each day he grew closer to her.

When he would return home from work

Gracie would be in the kitchen, putting the final touches on dinner. When he walked inside, Gracie would shriek with joy - "Johnny - you're home!" Then she would embrace him, holding him with desperate strength, as if he would be spirited away if she let go. And he held her back with equal urgency. She had become a part of him.

Later than evening, after dinner, they went to bed together.

They never had sex. He still saw her as child-like, even if not a child. She needed John, needed his strength, stability, and love. The age difference was still an issue with him. But when he would broach the subject, Gracie would smile and gently place her forefinger on his lips and he would lapse into a giddy silence.

Gracie loved to position herself when they were in bed by hugging John's back in a spooning position. John was not one to toss and turn, and he usually had no difficulty in falling asleep. John had a dream as he slept. He dreamed that he was staring up as he lay in bed, eyes wide open. The ceiling seemed different, wavering as if fluid. Then, it parted, opening itself to the night.

The stars were enormous, pulsing like neon. Then, descending from the night's bold glow, came an angel.

Her wings moved slowly as she lowered herself. Then he saw - it was an angel who looked like Gracie, gliding downward until she was sitting on top of him, moving up and down upon him, sweeping him into rapture.

Then he awoke. But the angel travelled with him outside the dream, moving with heat and urgency. It was Gracie. They were locked together, moving fierce and strong as lovers do until the dawn brought them stillness.

Gracie looked into John's eyes. "Johnny, when I was a little girl, I would dream about you - before we ever met. But I knew, if I could just hold on, someday you would come and save me. I love you Johnny."

Johnny kissed Gracie around her eyes. She was beautiful; a beautiful woman with a child's innocence. A tear fell from his eye and joined a tear from Gracie's cheek, becoming one. "And I love you, Gracie, and I will never let go of you. I want us to be together always."

And so it went. They were married in the small town's chapel. John wanted to take Gracie on a honeymoon - a Caribbean cruise, or a couple of weeks in Paris, but she was not interested. She wanted to be with John in their home.

And in the summer, one evening as they sat

on the swing lounge in the veranda, amidst the swirl of fireflies and beneath the canopy of stars, John placed his hand on the growing swell of Gracie's belly.

And he remembered the fortune cookie. It came to light. He really did not know what hit him.

And he never regretted forgetting to duck.

Diversity

Jack had been walking aimlessly on this hot October evening, not noticing he had wandered into an unfamiliar part of town. He was on a dark, quiet street, so empty of people it seemed like curfew was in effect. Then he saw the sign- THE WELCOME ALL TAVERN, shining in bold neon. His throat was dry- he was thirsty- he walked in.

He was nearly bowled over by the wide swath of diversity among the customers. It was as if every conceivable type of person, the full rainbow of humanity, was inside. All races, genders, ages and people with various abnormalities were assembled. Having always been an outsider himself, he felt drawn to the people who were the oddest.

He scanned the tavern from corner to corner. At one table a dwarf wearing a gold tuxedo chatted amiably with a seven-foot-tall albino man with long blue dreadlocks. At another table a blind man was reading Tarot cards to a one legged rabbi. Another table- a particularly thick, sturdy one- featured a 500-pound ballerina twirling daintily with graceful precision. Off in a corner, a man wearing a jockey's cap and a g-string wielded a riding crop while astride a rocking horse that was too small for a toddler. "Hop on, cowboy, always room for one more!" the jockey said to Jack. Flustered a bit, Jack moved on.

In the center of the tavern a bald woman wearing a vintage dress was holding court before a small group consisting of three nuns, a dominatrix, and a man wearing a welder's mask. Jack couldn't help but to notice that her forehead was receding, her head narrowed on top and her dark eyes were set very close together. She smiled at Jack and beckoned him over.

"I couldn't help notice you staring at me," she told Jack. "My name is Lilly. I have microcephaly. Isn't it terrible how society stereotypes. I bet you assumed I was challenged- an idiot perhaps. But

I'm really quite bright. Would you care to join us? My friends and I were discussing Copernicus and the space/time continuum."

Jack politely demurred and walked to the bar for a beer. The bartender was a big man with a flannel shirt and a lumberjack's beard. His name was Gus.

"I really like this place," Jack told Gus. "So many different, interesting people."

Gus smiled. "Just like the sign says- welcome all. Everybody- and I mean everybody- is welcome here."

Jack sipped his beer, then noticed a man slumped over at the end of the bar. He looked, well, more normal than the others, but he was not moving at all. In fact, it looked like he wasn't even breathing. "Is something wrong with that man?" Jack asked Gus.

"Oh him," Gus replied. "That's the dead guy."

Jack searched Gus' face for droll humor or sarcasm. There was none. "The dead guy?" queried Jack.

"Yeah," Gus replied nonchalantly. "The dead guy. He doesn't bother anyone. You saw the sign- we don't turn anyone away."

"But-but a dead guy?" asked Jack. "How long has he been here?"

"Oh, I don't know," replied Gus. "Maybe a month-two months. I don't keep track of these things. He's welcome here, just like everyone else."

"But- a dead guy? Doesn't he smell bad?"

"Evidently not," replied Gus. "Haven't heard any complaints. He looks like a decent fellow- why don't you have a beer with him?"

Jack felt his head flush. He made a beeline for the exit.

Lilly spoke as he walked by. "Leaving already, handsome? We were about to discuss Descartes and the mind/body dichotomy. Join us."

The door swung wide and Jack hit the streets. He walked toward the main drag, where the familiar sounds of traffic and the sight of normal people doing normal things would be calming, where there was safety and conformity.

Then he stopped. The October wind hit his face. He turned around and walked back to the tavern. It was a perfect night to discuss Descartes with the smart lady- and the dead guy really did seem like a decent fellow.

Mr. Snail

"You can go outside, David, but don't go far; stay in the yard and don't go outside the fence."

Mommy takes such good care of me. But sometimes I wish I could go a little bit outside the gate. I remember once when the gate was left open I went out just a little ways to visit my friends, Mr. Squirrel and Mr. Snail. Mr. Squirrel is funny and has great big dark eyes and a bushy tail. When he comes inside the fence, Mommy lets me feed him nuts. He can stand on his hind legs and hold the nut with his front feet. I like to watch his bushy tail wiggle when he nibbles on the nuts. Once when I was sitting on the grass, Mr. Squirrel jumped on my lap and I fed him a nut that I held in my hand. It tickled when he nibbled and his bushy tail wiggled back and forth. Mr. Squirrel is a good friend.

Mr. Snail is my best friend. Sometimes when I play outside all by myself I get lonely. And then Mr. Snail appears like magic. His face is different from Mr. Squirrel's, and his eyes are on long stems that slowly move around this way and that. That's how he talks to me, with his eyes. I always listen very closely; Mr. Snail sees many things and is very wise.

"David- come inside. Lunch is ready!"

Mommy makes the best lunches. She makes sandwiches with dark bread because dark bread is healthier than white. My favorite sandwich is peanut butter and jelly. And she makes soups with lots of vegetables, and there is a different fruit every day. My favorite dessert is oatmeal cookies. Mommy bakes them herself and they are big and round. Sometimes, if I've been good, I get to have two.

We eat lunch together every day. I like to look at the pictures on the wall when we eat. There are pictures of trees and lakes and different people. One picture confuses me. It's a picture of Mommy with a tall man. Mommy looks very pretty and is wearing a white dress that goes down to her ankles, and she is holding a bunch of flowers in her hand. Mommy and the man look so happy together; I've never seen her so happy.

"Mommy, who is that man with you in that picture?"

Mommy looks sad. There are tears in her eyes. I don't like to see her sad.

Mommy chokes a little, then answers. "That's you, David. Sometimes you can remember, and sometimes you forget. That was the happiest day of my life, sweetheart. That's the day we were married. And we were happy for several years, then something sad happened. There was a big boom inside your head called a stroke. And now, most of the time, you can only remember being a little boy. But sometimes the boom goes away and, for at least a little while, you're a grown man again. But you must always remember, whether you're a grown up or a little boy, Mommy loves you very much and will always be with you."

One day I was playing in the yard. It was the October month. Everything around me glowed, bright and golden. The trees beyond the fence were alive, bright yellow and red. Oh, if only I could go beyond the fence and play where the trees were. They were dancing and making crackling sounds in the breeze.

I wonder if I can go outside the fence if Mommy comes with me. I'll ask her and promise to be twice as good if she lets me play in the trees. The trees are so pretty in the October time. I like to watch the leaves go back and forth when they fall and float to the ground.

I go inside the house and Mommy is in the kitchen. It smells so good- she's baking oatmeal cookies! I'm going to ask her if we can go outside the fence when she finishes. Then there is a white light all around me and a boom inside my head.

I wake up on the floor. My head is nestled on a woman's lap.

"Sarah- oh god Sarah- is it really you?" She holds my head to her breast and kisses my face, then helps me to my feet. I hold her to me, so tight I can hear her heart beating. We kiss- we can't stop just like when we were teenagers. I feel heat, pulsing and moving to my groin.

"How long this time, Sarah? How long was I the child?"

"Oh David- it was just over three weeks, which is an improvement. The neurologist told me that if the times you are little David are briefer with each episode, the odds improve that you will at some point be as you are now permanently."

We embrace again. Sarah takes me by the hand, and we go to our bedroom. How long has it been? I can't remember. We make love. Sarah's passion seems strange, almost violent in intensity. Her arms and legs pull me into her, and even when we finish she doesn't let go, as if to capture me as I am now and not allow the child to return.

We dress and talk. I want to know how she manages; does she get lonely when I'm a child? What do I say when I'm the child?

"You make friends with some of the animals who come inside the fence. You speak to them and believe they speak back. You're becoming more assertive. The doctor thinks this is a good sign— that it may mean you are struggling unconsciously to return to your adult state. But it worries me. Of late, you've been wanting to go beyond the fence, out into the woods to play among the Autumn trees. October has always been your favorite month. But I don't want you to, David, not even if I'm with you."

"But what if it might make me more confident and self-reliant? What if it might help me stay as I am now?"

"Let's discuss this more tomorrow, sweetheart. I want you to hold me- I want to fall asleep in your arms."

"Yes Sarah. Hold me tight. I'm your husband, not your child. Don't let me get away."

My head hurts. Something is pounding in my head. Where am I? Why am I in bed with Mommy? This feels funny- strange. I feel excited being in bed with Mommy. I'm big below my stomach. I don't understand. This doesn't seem right. I should get up and put on my clothes.

I'm dressed. I want to go outside.

I'm in the yard, inside the fence. I want to go outside the fence where the trees are, but I don't want to disobey Mommy.

A butterfly! A big pretty butterfly. It's flying toward the trees.

I'm going to go outside the fence, only a little ways, to find the butterfly. Mommy's still asleep. As soon as I find the butterfly, I'll come back inside the fence before Mommy wakes up.

I lift the latch on the gate. I have a funny feeling, kind of like when I woke up in bed with Mommy. Then, I walk outside the fence toward the big trees with their golden hair of leaves.

I see it again! Such a pretty butterfly, dancing in loops through the trees. His wings are red and golden, like the leaves. I start to run, zig zagging through the trees, just like the butterfly zig zags in the air. The October time colors are everywhere, on the ground and in the trees and I feel happy and free. I never want to stay inside the fence again.

I run and I run, trying to stay up with the butterfly, going farther and farther away from the fence and deeper into the October place where the trees get bigger and bigger and the golden red leaves, shiny from the sun, rain down on me.

Where is the butterfly? He has flown away, lost in flight in the golden sky.

I've run too much. I stop to rest and sit on the ground, the ground covered with a thick carpet of golden leaves. The leaves make crackling sounds when I sit and are warm and smell good and I am happy.

I think it's time to go back home, inside the fence. Mommy might be awake now and will worry if she can't find me.

I stand up and look around where I am, and suddenly I'm confused. I'm confused and scared. How far did I run? I don't know where I am.

I sit back down on the crackling ground, covered and thick with brittle leaves that break beneath me.

Which way should I go? I don't like this feeling. This lost feeling where I don't know which way to go.

I'm scared and lonely. I feel lost and all alone. My cheeks start to tremble and tears are in my eyes. The tears are big and feel warm on my cheeks. I'm not supposed to- not supposed to cry. Big boys don't cry, but I'm lost and alone and start to cry.

I hear something near me. I hear leaves crackling near me, but the sound is faint and slow. I look around. What is making that sound? I bend my head, close to the ground and I see something- something small and slow, crawling toward me through the crackling leaves.

It's Mr. Snail!

Mr. Snail stops crawling and is near my knee. His long eyes wiggle at me. Mr. Snail is kind and wise and is my friend.

"Help me, Mr. Snail. I'm lost and I want to go home. I want to go back inside the fence and be with Mommy."

Mr. Snail hears me. He talks to me with his eyes and wants to help. Mr. Snail knew where I was and crawled all this way to help me.

He turns his head and his long eyes stop wiggling and are straight and stiff. Mr. Snail is pointing in the direction I must go to find my way home. Mr. Snail is kind and wise and he is my friend. I will walk in the direction I must go to find my way home. Mr. Snail is kind and wise and he is my friend. I will walk in the direction he points to with his eyes that speak to me and tell me what to do.

I start to walk. I am following the path Mr. Snail has set for me and with each step I hear him speak. He is telling me that I can't be a little boy anymore, and that it is time. My head feels clearer and with each step I feel bigger and less confused. I hear every word Mr. Snail speaks and he is wise, and he is my friend. He tells me I am a man, a man named David, who is the husband of Sarah, who is not my Mommy but the wife I love dearly and must return to. He tells me I am at childhood's end, and there is a flash inside my head and I can see home and Sarah running toward me and Mr. Snail is wise and he is my friend and I am a man named David who loves a woman named Sarah- I am a man named David and will remain a man named David and I will love Sarah forever as a man would love her , and Mr. Snail is wise and there will never be turning back.

Treading on Hallowed Ground

"I assume, Mr. Dubois, you have heard the expression, "Money is no object?"

Simon Dubois listened with a mildly amused expression on his face. He was a six feet, five inch black man in his early thirties, green eyed, suave and impeccably attired. Although lithe and sinewy, there was a vague, androgynous quality to his appearance. He bore an essential ambiguity - as if he were a strange and formidable hybrid.

He was sitting in the office of Alden Channing, CEO of the Universal Solutions Corporation. Channing was a dour, mildly obese man in his late fifties, his graying hair parted unfashionably down the middle.

"Yes," he continued, "I would think that most people would dismiss that expression as a cliched hyperbole. But, in truth, as times and fortunes have grown unrestrained, there are those for whom money is quite literally no object. These people have wealth that would render the Fortune 500 paupers by comparison. They move through society, clandestine and invisible. They get what they want with impunity, removed from the constraints of law and morality. Think if you will of children who behave on impulse. They see something shiny, and grab it, unbridled of fear or conscience. And they never go away empty handed."

Dubois listened, implacable and intent on studying the man who was speaking to him. He studied his body language and gestures. He had learned to measure the other person's state of mind and emotion through the number of breaths taken per minute. Vocal inflection was always a sure measurement of both fear and honesty. He was sure Channing was not aware of it himself, but his eyes would change focus every few seconds and his gaze would drift toward the coiled tendrils of Dubois' long, flaring dreadlocks. Other men could afford such distractions, but in

Dubois' line of work even a fleeting distraction could be fatal. Channing paused, took a deep breath, and wet his lips. Then he continued.

"When the people I've described encounter obstacles to what they desire, they often consult with a company such as mine. Then, if a last resort becomes necessary, we subcontract with an expert - someone with credentials nonpareil - someone like you."

Channing pressed a button on his desk and a large screen appeared on the wall. Then an image came into focus. It was an aerial picture of a large, majestic old house set upon a bluff with a panoramic view of an ocean.

"What you're looking at, Mr. Dubois, is a property my client must acquire, and money is no object.

The subject property is contained on roughly fifty acres of level, buildable land, improved by an exceptionally well-maintained house of twenty two thousand square feet, which does not include extensive basement area. The improvement was built in 1858, but contains modern amenities. There are two smaller improvements on the site, as well as a large barn. Much of the site is heavily wooded, but if desired the trees could be removed and additional improvements could be built. From a market standpoint, the property's most valuable feature is its unencumbered panoramic ocean view. There may not be a superior ocean view on the entire east coast."

Channing paused in his presentation and wet his lips. "Are there any questions at this time, Mr. Dubois?

"No," replied Dubois." Not at this time."

Channing again ran his tongue across his lips, then continued.

"The owner of the property is named Terrence Harper. The property has vested in his family for multiple generations. He is a man in his late sixties, and in his youth was a bit of an adventurer and soldier of fortune. He is a man of no small means himself, apparently through inheritance.

At some point in his late thirties, he developed an interest in his genealogy and his ancestors' connection to the property. Our sources indicate he concurrently studied, and became obsessed with, arcane, pre-Christian religions and cults. He subsequently cloistered himself away in the house and has become a near recluse."

Channing looked at Dubois. He appeared to be listening intently, but there was an oddness in his lack of movement. When he began his presentation, Dubois was sitting in a conference chair, his legs crossed and arms at his sides, and nearly a half hour later he had not moved an inch.

"Questions - observations, Mr. Dubois?"

"No," he replied, still displaying an expression of mild amusement. "No, Mr. Channing, not yet."

"Our representatives have reached out to Mr. Harper, explaining there is a highly motivated buyer who wants to purchase his property. Oh, by the way, did I mention the estimated fair market value of the property?"

"No, you did not," replied Dubois.

"The property is estimated to be worth eighty million dollars. We offered him - 1.5 billion. An offer, as they say, he could not refuse. Well, he refused it. He refused the offer and told us he would not sell for any price. Period."

"And to what would you ascribe Mr. Harper's intractability?" asked Dubois.

"Harper is a man of peculiar spiritual beliefs. This may be the result of his religious studies. He believes the property is sacred and all of his lineage have been its protectors. He believes he is the gatekeeper of hallowed land."

Channing paused and opened a drawer in his desk. He extracted a tube of lip balm and applied a dab onto his lips. Then he smiled and continued.

"Solutions, Mr. Dubois, that is what my associates and I sell - solutions.

We have discovered that Harper has no immediate family, nor does he have a will. But our research has uncovered two individuals who are his grand nephews. If Harper were to pass on, through the laws of succession, these grand nephews would inherit the property. These heirs have been discreetly queried, and we have full assurance they do not share any of their grand uncle's spiritual beliefs. They are quite enthusiastically receptive to an offer which is extravagantly generous. Do you have any questions, Mr. Dubois?"

For the first time, Dubois shifted position in his chair. "Yes," he replied, "but only a few."

"Please, Mr. Dubois, I am eagerly at your disposal."

"The property you have described is quite sprawling. Does Harper employ any individuals in the role of security?"

"None whatever, Mr. Dubois. The only staff in Harper's employ are two groundskeepers. Harper prefers to allow most of the land to remain feral. The house, of course, is enormous, but only a relatively small portion is used by its lone occupant. Harper does have food and various sundries delivered on a weekly basis, always on Wednesday."

"How far from the property is the nearest town?"

"Twenty miles, a very small burgh called Ravensloft, population less than 300."

Dubois stood up. Channing had forgotten the height of the man.

"I want $500,000.00 before I depart on this assignment. When my obligation on our oral contract has been consummated, my fee will be an additional one million dollars."

Channing extended his hand. "Excellent, Mr. Dubois - excellent. Now go forth, and prepare the property for sale."

Simon Dubois was a meticulous man. After his meeting with Channing, he made arrangements to have his working vehicle, a black, rebuilt 1985 Jaguar E-type, shipped to Portsmouth, New Hampshire from his home in Key West. Perhaps it was in part superstition, but he no longer felt in complete control driving anything else. The shipment would take about a week. In the interim, he would study - topographical and aerial maps and photos, projected weather forecasts, the prevalence and behavior of area state troopers (a well dressed black man with dreadlocks, driving a loaded Jaguar in an isolated stretch of New England would likely present both curiosity and temptation to law enforcement.) He selected from a collection of counterfeit I.D and credit cards, and documents confirming his front occupation as an I.T. consultant. He placed fifty thousand dollars from his upfront payment into a money belt. Far more money that he would probably need for bribes and expenses, but the unexpected could always happen. And, finally, his weapons. He shouldn't need much for this job: a Glock 19 with suppressor, a Beretta 70, and a vintage stiletto. When strapped to Dubois' ankle, it became a sort of talisman - a cold, deadly rabbit's foot. All of the weapons fit neatly into a foolproof secret compartment in the Jaguar.

Dubois arrived in Portsmouth a day after his car. He checked into a Travel Lodge hotel (fortunately his expensive tastes didn't include lodging) and early morning the next day he would make the hundred and twenty mile drive to, as Channing liked to describe it, the subject property.

It was the first week of October, cool but not cold, perfect driving weather. The music of John Coltrane flowed through his earbuds as he drove, the Jaguar slicing through the miles on the sparsely trafficked highway. There was something about driving with few other vehicles on the road that appealed to him. It was nearly solipsistic in its insularity - contained in a fast moving vessel, where the absence of humanity rendered memories of people he had known into apparitions of imagination. He was hardly a man of introspection, but on long solitary drives the inevitable questions always reared up from within. How did he get here, and how did he come to be who he was? His own past sometimes seemed a figmentation - a chimera of questionable reality. He knew some of his personal history - a Haitian father, a Jamaican Irish mother. But he never knew them.

When he grew up in foster homes, he was only shown a few pictures of them and told they had died during a home robbery gone deadly, and their killer never noticed the sleeping infant in another room. But the story always had a tint of fabrication to him.

His foster parents were always kind to him, but never quite loving. Most of them were white, and he was home schooled much of the time. He never had difficulty learning things, and at one point he was deemed to be gifted; but what did that really mean?

In his late teens, he realized he was attractive

to most of the young women he encountered, as well as a large number of young men. He excelled at athletics and was given a full athletic scholarship to a prestigious college for his track and field abilities. When he graduated, he had degrees in both philosophy and economics, and was fluent in four languages. His future was promising and options numerous. Then, on one hot summer night, he discovered his true calling.

He had travelled from his home in Baltimore to New Orleans to sample the city's jazz clubs. This was to be a brief post graduation fling before being interviewed for a job with a tech firm. He was drinking in one of the clubs and, between sets, he noticed a large white man with a baleful demeanor staring at him. He made little of it at first, but it soon became apparent the man was fixated on him.

After the last set, he rose and walked out of the club, immediately followed by the man who had stared at him so intently. The footsteps grew louder, then he heard a deep, drunken voice shout, "Turn around - Police!"

Dubois turned around. The man was tall and heavyset, and beads of sweat poured down his round, porcine face. In one hand he held a N.O.P.D badge, in the other a gun.

"Alright, dreadlocks, step behind this building."

Dubois complied, surprised by his own lack of fear. When the two of them were out of sight from the main drag, the cop stepped close to Dubois, inches from his face. His breath reeked of hatred and bourbon. "You like watching other niggers blowing on horns? Well now this nigger gets to practice on my horn. You know the drill, pretty boy - down on your knees."

Dubois appeared passive as he complied, dropping to his knees.

Putting his badge in his pocket, the cop fumbled with his zipper while keeping his gun trained on Dubois. Then, it all happened so quickly.

Dubois felt detached from his own body as if a spectator. He watched himself, as he grabbed the cop's gun with one hand and punched him in his groin with the other. There was a bellow of pain from the cop, his eyes wide with shock. This was not supposed to happen. It had been so easy in the past, an off duty recreation and a perk of the job.

The two men struggled, their shadows entwined, dancing against the building in the dim light. Dubois twisted the cop's wrist, and he heard a crack. The gun came loose and was now in his hand.

Using the gun as a bludgeon, he began pounding his adversary's head. The cop dropped to his knees as Dubois continued striking his head, hard, and without respite.

What was once a man's head was now a crushed, bloodied mass.

He put the gun in his jacket pocket, then looked around the building's corner for witnesses. There were none.

He then walked, careful to not look in haste, back to his hotel. With each step he expected to feel something. To feel some change, be it fear, remorse, triumph or relief. There was nothing. His breathing was steady, his pulse slow and even. It was as if nothing had happened, no different in substance from countless other things that had happened and continued to happen, as the din and madness of the French Quarter grew faint with each succeeding step. He didn't believe in destiny, but he knew what he was destined to be.

It was near dusk as he saw the sign: Ravensloft - 20 miles ahead.

As he approached the town's outskirts, Dubois noticed a stand alone building just ahead. The structure was spare and rustic. A sign, glowing incongruously in neon was above the entrance: The Goat's Horn Tavern.

He pulled into the parking lot and got out of the car. He was now wearing his working clothes. All items were black - his denim slacks, pull over sweater and leather jacket. His guns were holstered snuggly beneath his jacket, his stiletto sheathed to his ankle.

When he entered the tavern, he was taken aback by the ambience and decor. The interior was in bold contrast to the stark, rudimentary design of the exterior.

The walls were painted with stylized floral designs blended with the clear lines and geometric shapes of classic Deco. The tables and chairs appeared circa nineteen thirties, with ebony and ivory inlays, and the bar counter was long and sleek, made of highly polished mahogany with flourishes of silver, black, and chrome.

The atmosphere appealed to Dubois' sensibilities, which leaned toward the retro. Then, he noticed the bartender.

He stood behind the bar, a man in his fifties with an odd pallor which stood in contrast to his slicked back, jet black hair. He wore a gunmetal grey silk suit with no tie, and the rest of him was hidden below the bar. With a small flicker of a smile, he welcomed Dubois.

"Good evening, Sir, and welcome. May I offer you a drink? With strangers, the first one is always on the house."

"Thank you," replied Dubois. "I'll have a scotch, straight up." He continued to survey the bar as his drink was poured. He noticed a lack of photographs or other memorabilia connected to customers. He was, in fact, the sole customer.

The bartender handed him his drink. He took a sip. It was excellent scotch. He was expecting to taste a mediocre house brand.

"I compliment you on the decor," he told the bartender. "This degree and quality of Deco rivals the best I've seen in New York or Paris. Perhaps I've underestimated the sensibilities of rural New England."

The bartender smiled. "No, you haven't been unkind to rural New England. This decor is highly atypical. One of a kind for our region - our neck of the woods, so to speak. What you see reflects the taste of the owner, Mr. Harper."

"Terrence Harper?" asked Dubois. "Yes, he lives in the huge old house on the bluff about twenty miles from here. He's a strange man with a lot of money. He used to come down and drink here from time to time; now he is seldom seen. He's become a bit of a hermit. Do you know him?"

"We have never met, but I'm here for a meeting with him. My name is David Crenshaw. I'm an I.T. consultant. Apparently, Mr. Harper's computers have exhausted their shelf lives. He wants to upgrade and possibly have a security system installed on his property."

The bartender's eyes darted to the side, almost imperceptibly. Dubois felt a chill, like an ice cube drawn down his spine. The bartender's face seemed to flush, losing its pallor. "May I freshen your drink-Mr. Dubois?"

Before the final syllable escaped the bartender's lips, Dubois had stepped to his side and spun around.

There were two of them, one with a long blade in his hand, the other with a length of piano wire.

Dubois' reaction was a blend of reflex and practiced choreography. He moved to the flank of the one who was set to garrote him with the piano wire, using him as a shield against the man with the knife. As the piano wire was raised and the man's arms were above his head, he grabbed him by his wrists and bore down. The sound of breaking bones was followed by a scream. The he shoved the man toward his knife wielding cohort, knocking him off balance. In a heartbeat, Dubois reached to his ankle and drew the stiletto. The knife wielder lunged at Dubois, his long blade reflecting the light from an overhead chandelier. With a click, Dubois' own blade uncoiled. The man lunged again, but he was too slow. Dubois' parried and thrust his knife into the man's heart. The broken armed man writhed on the floor. Dubois bent over and slit his throat. His last breath sounded like a child's toy rattle.

The bartender had a club in his hand, then, realizing the futility, dropped it behind the bar. He was approached by Dubois.

"How did you know my name?" The bartender showed no fear. "Information flows in ways you can't imagine. We were expecting you, although not quite this soon."

"I can imagine almost anything. I'll repeat the question. You stated my name. How did you know?"

"Through the grapevine, Mr. Dubois - the grapevine."

Dubois knew he would get nothing from him. There was no time to apply persuasion.

He removed the Glock from beneath his jacket and attached the suppressor. "Any closing thoughts?"

"Yes - in the form of advice. Kill me, or let me live, either way. But there's still time – turn back."

Dubois took aim between the bartender's eyes. "I never turn back."

"Then your fate is sealed, heretic. You will be treading on hallowed ground."

He pulled the trigger, then was gone.

Dark of night had fallen as he drove. He decided to bypass the town of Ravensloft, as charming as it may be. He reassessed his situation - his assignment. He knew he no longer needed to be concerned about law enforcement. Recluse or not, Harper did not exist in a vacuum. He cast a wide shadow beyond the seclusion of his insular compound. The men at the bar, the people of Ravensloft - these were his people, willing to kill or die for him. He doubted that law enforcement ventured into Harper's domain.

The full moon cast enough light that he had a clear view of the passing landscape. He saw upright stones, some tabled with horizontal stones, menhirs and dolmens. They were identical to the Stone Age monuments of the ancient Celts, and they became more numerous the closer he got to Harper.

The road narrowed and twisted, and suddenly he was there.

He pulled over and got out of the car. There it was, on top of the bluff: Harper's fortress - the subject property.

The night was still and silent as Dubois climbed the twisted cobbled pathway leading up to the house. He now had to resort to an alternate plan. Speed and stealth were now paramount. Both he and Channing had miscalculated. If Harper was a recluse, alone and unsuspecting, within twenty minutes he would have been driving back to Portsmouth. Now he must wait.

Near the top of the pathway he found a nook behind some shrubs where he would be concealed. From near the top of the bluff, he could see for miles around. He waited. After fifteen minutes, he saw there was no one on the road in pursuit. Either it was a slow night at the tavern and the bodies had not yet been discovered, or the grapevine the bartender alluded to hit a snag.

Now for the entry. A window? Perhaps down through the wine cellar? Or, perhaps the Occam's Razor theory was apropos, and simply walk through the front door?

He went with Occam's Razor.

Climbing the steep steps to the front porch, he paused as he faced the door. It was thick and wide, oaken and with a very old brass door handle. He pressed down on the latch and there was no resistance. It was unlocked. A trap? His instincts told him no.

He opened the door and walked inside.

It was just like the tavern, the decor, the furnishings, the art - all a homage to Art Deco. He reached inside his jacket and extracted the Glock. Now, to find Harper. If he were hiding, locating him within the immense area might present a challenge. Then he heard the voice.

"Welcome, Mr. Dubois. I've been awaiting you."

He knew Harper was close although he remained unseen. The voice sounded mere feet away.

"Before you consummate your contact with Mr. Channing, please allow the condemned man a few words before bidding adieu to the Vale of Tears."

"Show yourself, Harper. I would never refuse a man his farewell address, if given in good faith. Being a killer and being honorable are not mutually exclusive."

Harper stepped out from behind a curtain. It was almost as if he appeared from behind a magician's cloak.

Dubois looked at him. He was tall - almost as tall as himself, and slender. His graying hair was of medium length, and although pale, his face bore a craggy appearance and was lined; the face of a man who kept indoors, but once weathered the elements and the effronteries of experience.

"You needn't worry about the clock. You have no pursuers, Mr. Dubois. The unpleasantness you encountered at the tavern was not per my instruction. Overzealous supporters of mine took it upon themselves to head you off at the pass. They underestimated your mettle. Now they are dead."

"And what did you want to say to me before the curtain closes, Harper?"

"May we sit, Mr. Dubois? And would you object to my having a brandy? Would you care for a drink?"

"Thank you. Scotch, straight up."

Harper prepared the drinks and handed the scotch to Dubois, then the two men sat down on a pair of black velvet Deco chairs.

"Let me go back to the origins, Mr. Dubois. And by the way, there really is a grapevine, and I am aware of some of the things Channing told you in your meeting."

Harper paused and sipped his brandy. Dubois wondered where this was all going. Would it culminate in an argument as to why he should be spared? It would not be the first time, and it had never worked before.

"During the Bronze Age - long before the Norsemen set foot on North America, my ancestors arrived on these shores, within sight from where we now sit.

They were Celtic people, from Northern Europe. There is some ambiguity whether they arrived here by design or through happenstance. You undoubtedly saw some of their megaliths en route to my home.

These settlers, unlike other Europeans who colonized centuries later, enjoyed harmony and shared beliefs with the native peoples. Both groups believed that there was a higher power manifest in nature and that Earth, the Mother, was alive and should be revered. Everything was alive and sentient; the forest and the rivers, the mountains and rocks, the dirt itself beneath their feet, was alive. They believed that there were many gods for the many things within the sky above and the ground below.

Then the Puritans, centuries later, arrived. The hateful Puritans, with their belief in a single, psychotic god and that they should have domain over the Earth and all of her flora and fauna. They believed that the pleasures of the flesh were evil and hell fire and damnation awaited all who were in disagreement.

Conflict between the Celts and their kindred souls the Native people and the Puritans was inevitable, then conflict escalated to war. Holy war.

Not long after the Puritans arrival, slave ships bearing human cargo from Africa reached our shores. The Puritans stripped them of their humanity, and they were treated like animals, forced to do slave labor. Any resistance on their part was met with punishments too draconian to describe. But the slaves were strong both in body and spirit, and rebellions were inevitable. Many slaves from the South escaped and joined their comrades in the North East. They were hunted down and many gravitated here, on the land where we now sit. Yes, Mr. Dubois, there is a grapevine, and they heard through that grapevine that they would receive protection and succor from the Celts and Native people who occupied this sacred land."

Dubois looked at his watch. "I agreed to listen to some final words, not an entire treatise on race relations in the New World. This is turning into a filibuster."

Harper sipped his brandy and smiled. "Hardly a stream of meaningless words designed to burn time, Mr. Dubois. Please be patient for a bit longer. My conclusion will come soon.

The Puritans organized and began their pursuit. They had superior weapons in firearms, rudimentary as they were. But their most powerful weapon was their hatred. We represented everything that was contrary to what they believed, and they were hell bent on our genocide. Then, our three groups: Celtic, Native people, and African joined forces and forged a sacred bond on this bluff where this house would be built some two centuries later.

As the Puritans amassed forces below, the priests, priestesses, and shamans convened. They prayed and chanted to the various gods and spirits they had worshipped for millennia. There appeared a sign in the heavens. It loomed above like a fire in the sky. The sign was a three-pointed star, with each point curved like a scythe.

All of the assembled began to chant and pray, then a thunderclap exploded in the sky and they were silenced. Then, lightning struck, and they fell, stunned and in shock.

When they regained their senses they looked upon one another and saw that they bore the sign - the mark. Behind the left ear of all of them, small, but clearly delineated, was the three-pointed star.

And they all knew that they were blessed and protected, and they kissed the sacred ground on which they kneeled. And the ground spoke to them, and they heard, and knew that the ground would forever be cursed to anyone without the sacred mark, and all who would trespass with ill will would be struck dead.

And so it was. As the Puritans ascended the bluff they died instantly, and soon their bodies were stacked like cordwood below. After three days their bodies were burned as an offering, and the noonday sky turned black as coal and the land on which the ashes lay was salted."

"Well," replied Dubois, "I must be wearing magic shoes since I'm still here and I came with ill will - about as ill as it gets."

He removed his Glock from beneath his jacket and nonchalantly attached the suppressor.

"It's been a pleasure talking with you and your words will long be remembered. And with that…"

"Wait - one more minute Mr. Dubois. You may time me if you wish."

Dubois moaned. Why am I humoring him? This isn't like me. Maybe it's time for a career change.

"Do you know, Mr. Dubois, you have

magnificent dreadlocks? They flow majestically down over your ears and past your shoulders."

Dubois was incredulous. After his long metaphysical pitch he was resorting to flattery as a final Hail Mary?

"My final entreaty, Mr. Dubois." Harper had a mirror in his hand with a Deco motif handle. Had Harper played his cards right he should have discussed his passion for Deco - a passion they both shared, Dubois mused.

"Take this mirror and look beneath your lovely tassels behind your left ear. And then, if you wish, shoot me."

Should he allow this one final indulgence? What harm in it? One last granted request, but only because Harper had exquisite taste.

He raised his locks and held the mirror to this left ear. He had to twist his neck to see. It was there. He turned and looked back at Harper. He was now standing and he turned his head to his right. The three pointed star; the points curved like sharpened blades.

Dubois tried to speak. "How…"

"The mark appeared as soon as you set foot on this hallowed land. How much do you know about yourself, Mr. Dubois? You grew up a virtual orphan. Do you truly know your lineage - your roots?"

"My - my parents were murdered when I was an infant. My father was a Haitian; my mother was mixed raced - Jamaican Irish. I was raised in foster homes. So much of my childhood is a blur - a strange blend of memories of other memories."

"The grapevine, Mr. Dubois. It's alive, and breathes and exhales knowledge. I've been aware of you for many years, long before your flamboyant appearance at the tavern. I've been aware of you, and expecting you since before you were born.

You mentioned your mixed race; African and Irish. The Celtic people who settled here were predominantly from what would later become Ireland. But there is an even richer aspect to your mix. There is also Native American.

Yes, your parents were murdered. But not during a burglary that escalated. They were murdered protecting you. Their killers weren't burglars; they were assassins sent to murder you."

Dubois held the mirror up behind his left ear again, as if not believing his eyes the first time. But the mark was still there. If anything, it now appeared more prominent, larger than the one behind Harper's ear.

"Why, Harper? Why would they want me

dead?"

"You, Mr. Dubois, are a part of our lore, of our oral tradition. Only a select few of us, and a select few of our oppressors, knew that a champion was destined to be born, in the year in which you were born. The oppressors found you before we did. Your parents fought heroically for you, and the ensuing commotion drew the police before the assassins could murder you. Then we intervened. We successfully broke the trail leading to you by arranging that you be cared for by a series of white foster parents to obfuscate your whereabouts. As I mentioned, only a select few knew of your identity. Quite obviously, the tavern keeper and your fellow patrons, were not a part of the select few.

Have you ever analyzed your superiority? Your propensity for violence and contempt for convention? You are descended from the most formidable of all the rebellious slaves. And you are also descended from the strongest and most willful of the Celts and Native people.

The war between ourselves and our oppressors, the true heretics, is a war between essential beliefs. It is a war that expanded from this bluff and its surrounding land to the world at large; a war without boundaries, fought clandestinely within the creases of shadows. The stakes are high; existential. The struggle is over the survival of the Earth herself. The heretics believe the Earth is theirs to exploit and plunder, to pillage and pollute. They believe in a hateful god- a god of irrational cruelty, a god of genocide, of plagues, wars and pestilence, and the heretics believe they are the anointed soldiers who must mete out this genocide on those of us who worship Mother Earth and revere all of her wonders. We are not the sinners and the heretics, Mr. Dubois; it is them. And you, whether you accept destiny or not, are the chosen one."

Dubois' mind went into overdrive. None of this was rational. Had he heard Harper's words yesterday they would be dismissed on face. Was he in the throes of a hallucination? Was this a dream? And if so, when did the dream begin? When he arrived at Harper's house? When he killed three men at the tavern? Or even earlier, when he met Channing?

"You mentioned Channing, Harper. What did your magic grapevine tell you about him?"

Harper smiled. "I've always known Channing, Mr. Dubois. He and his ancestors are in my bones, just as I and my ancestors are in his. So much in life is not as it seems. I know what he told you as if

I had been a fly on the wall. Money is no object; representing a shadow client of infinite wealth and influence, who is obsessed with acquiring this property. All fiction. You weren't sent here to dispatch me so the property could be sold by my heirs. You were sent because at this point in time I am equivalent to the high priest of my people. Channing is my analog for the heretics. You were duped, Mr. Dubois. Channing knows who you are - who you really are. Had he sent his own people, they would have perished the moment they set foot on hallowed ground. He knew you could do the job, impervious to the curse. Oh, what a coup it would have been - our champion - our chosen one - destroying the high priest, and, upon your return, your reception would be a deadly one. Two birds, Mr. Dubois, two birds with one stone."

Dubois walked to the wet bar and refreshed his drink. Then he took the mirror and looked again behind his ear. The mark was still there.

"And if it is true - if your fantastic narrative is true - what now?"

"Please come with me, Mr. Dubois. Please follow me outside."

The moon loomed above, enormous and blood red. Dubois followed Harper down a narrow path that led to the rear of the bluff. At the path's end was a small cemetery behind a wrought iron fence. Harper opened the gate and the two walked inside.

There were perhaps fifty tombstones, and two were off to the side, isolated from the others. They walked up to the headstones; the inscriptions clear beneath the bold moonlight:

Here lies
Jacob Harper
1602 – 1660
Wise and Loving
Father
To us all.

And beside it, the other headstone read:

Ezekiel Dubois
1605 - 1635
Fierce and Stalwart Brother
Rest In Peace and Rise Again.

"Our ancestors, Mr. Dubois - Simon. We are their direct descendants."

"And what...what if I choose not to join your struggle?"

"Our struggle, Simon. As you once mused, you may not believe in destiny, but you are destined."

"One question, Terence. Deco? We both have a passion for Deco. A coincidence?"

"It quite simply, Simon, is in our blood. And there are no coincidences."

The Jaguar sped down the empty highway. Dubois planned as he drove. He would arrive at Channing's office hours before it opened. Channing would not be alone. How many men would he have? It did not matter. He would bring his Uzi and get the jump on them. He was a killer. It was in his blood. He would save his people, and perhaps the Earth herself. His shadow would be long and deadly.

Heretics, beware.

Post Mortem Photography

It was an unusually warm October day in Willem Maryland as James Hundly loaded his photography equipment into the carriage.

It was 1886 and he thought about the reports he had heard of inventors and engineers who were on the verge of creating carriages that could be driven without horses. Progress. Progress seemed to be everywhere, especially in his business - photography. Newer technologies such as tintypes and calotypes were beginning to supplant the daguerreotype, but James was loyal to the technique mastered by Mathew Brady. James believed daguerreotypes, better than the newer technologies, captured the essence of death, as in Alexander Gardner's masterpiece images in "The Dead of Antietam." The essence of death. Death was the special niche James had settled into. He was an expert in his field - post mortem portrait photography.

On a warm day such as this one, he was grateful that the deceased on his latest assignment had passed only two days prior and wisely was placed on ice. During his career, he had accepted several assignments in which the deceased was left at room temperature and several days had elapsed postmortem. Copious amounts of perfume sprayed throughout the house could not begin to conceal the stench of death, and rigor mortis made the subject less pliable during the posing process.

The carriage pulled up to the large Victorian house on Dawson Street. James got off the carriage and, with assistance from the driver, toted his equipment up the steps to the front door. He gave the driver a generous gratuity, then tapped the door with the heavy brass knocker.

The door was opened by a woman. She appeared to be in her mid-forties and was attractive in spite of a harshness in her demeanor. Her eyes were cold and grey, and she was dressed in a black mourning gown that reached down to her ankles. Her dark hair was pulled back in a tight bun.

She extended her black gloved hand. "Mr. Hundly, my name is Leda Brown. I've explained the situation in detail in my letter. I am the mother of identical twin boys, Polux and Castor. They are twelve years of age. My dear Castor has departed our world of sorrows, leaving me only with Polux. Come with me into the parlor so I may introduce you."

"Yes - yes of course," replied James. "But first let me bring my equipment inside."

After moving the tools of his trade inside, he followed Mrs. Brown into the parlor. She walked with a decisive, almost frenetic gait. James had to step lively to keep pace with her.

When he entered the parlor, he saw them. Identical twins indeed, sitting side by side on an ornate burgundy divan.

They were handsome boys, blond, with delicately chiseled features. They wore matching outfits. Long sleeved white silk shirts with black bow ties. The sleeves were adorned with black pearl cufflinks. They were clad in knickerbocker knee pants with long white stockings. Their shoes were black leather, buffed to a glistening shine, with silver buckles. Somewhat incongruously, both wore white sailor caps, tilted ever so slightly toward their left eyes. The unevenness created an inadvertent appearance of rakishness.

"Boys, this is Mr. Hundly. He is an expert photographer, especially with subjects whose spirits have gone to another, happier realm."

James looked at the boys, a mirror image of one another. They both stared vacantly, their stillness unnerving. Were they both dead? Then, Polux blinked and turned his head toward James.

"Hello Mr. Hundly. My name is Polux." There was a gentle sweetness in his voice. He looked at his mother, then back at James. A plaintive apprehension registered in his eyes.

"Is that all you have to say to Mr. Hundly? Where are your manners?" Polux's mother was visibly agitated. "Is that all, Polux? You forgot to say, how are you? - You forgot to inquire as to Mr. Hundly's wellbeing."

James was becoming discomforted. Mrs. Brown's voice grew increasingly shrill with every syllable. "I taught you the same manners at the same time I taught your brother. Castor would never be so rude!" It was more a screech than a statement. She was teetering on the cusp of hysteria. Then, she grew calm and walked over to the divan and embraced Castor. "Oh, my poor baby," she cooed in his ear. "My poor, adorable baby." She held his head to her breast and gently stroked his cheek. "Mama still loves you, baby. Mama will always love you best." Her eyes teared as she carefully repositioned Castor, straightening a lock of his hair that had fallen out of place.

Mrs. Brown stood and smoothed her dress as she regained composure.

"You must forgive me, Mr. Hundly. These are difficult times for me. The times have always been difficult. I'm a widow, you know. My husband passed ten years ago, when my sons were only two. My poor, hapless Henry. His heart, dear man, had always been weak. You have no idea-a lone woman, trying her best to raise two boys. Boys can be difficult." She paused and glared at Polux. "Some boys."

"Well, Mrs. Brown," responded James, "it's not abnormal for young boys of your sons' age to have an abundance of energy and cause mischief. But it's usually harmless and they grow out of it. I've photographed dozens of boys who I was told were actually incorrigible, but once they are posed and under the lights, their misbehavior disappears." James paused and glanced at Castor and Polux. "Of course," he added, "misbehavior is not an issue with those boys who have escaped these earthly bounds."

Mrs. Brown continued to stare daggers at Polux, then her gaze softened as she turned her focus to Castor.

"All right, everyone, let's get started," announced James.

From his assembled items, James extracted a copper plate covered with silver, which he buffed to a glossy shine with a pad. He then slid the plate into the rear of the camera, which he then placed on a tripod. "Now Polux, sit closer to your brother. Look at his face. Look at the expression of peaceful calm projecting from his eyes. Now I want you to relax and try to look just like your brother, and hold that pose for about two minutes."

Polux turned his head and stared at Castor. He could not see calm or peacefulness. All he could see was death. Cold, unflinching death with vacant eyes that looked but could not see.

James placed the dark cloth hood over his head and made adjustments until the image before him was ready to be captured, photographically, for eternity. Then Polux abruptly sneezed.

"Now you've done it. Now you've ruined everything!" screamed Mrs. Brown.

"It's alright, Mrs. Brown. Nothing was harmed or damaged. We'll just start over at the beginning. I'm sure Polux sneezed because the air is growing stale."

"No, it's not alright!" shrieked Mrs. Brown. "All you needed to do, Polux, was keep still and look proper like your brother. All you had to do was be good for two minutes. Castor was good for twelve years, and you can't even muster two minutes of goodness!"

James looked at Polux. The poor boy. His situation was outlandish. Having to sit next to his dead identical twin was traumatic enough without his mother's venomous screech. The tenor of her wrath was bordering on mania. The look of fear and hurt on Polux's face was pitiful.

"Please, Mrs. Brown - try to contain yourself. Castor and Polux are identical twins. Everything about them, both physically and spiritually, is the same, and both were raised in the same household. If Castor was a good boy, then logically Polux must also be a good boy."

Mrs. Brown was scarlet and began to shake with rage. "He's not a good boy; he's bane. He's nothing like my sweet Castor except in appearance."

James felt that the situation was careening out

of control. He had seen the wide swath of human emotion in his line of work, but this was unique. The overt hatred of a mother for her son was terrifying and unnatural.

Mrs. Brown walked up to Polux. She was inches from his face. When she spoke, her words came as hisses, as if from an enraged viper.

"Castor was easy. He was gentle inside me, but you had to get twisted inside my womb. You ripped and tore me inside and made me useless!"

She began to scream like a lunatic banshee. Polux recoiled, and in doing so knocked Castor off the divan. "You monster!" she screamed. "You should be the dead one; you should have died at birth!"

Mrs. Brown knelt on the floor beside Castor and lifted him back in position on the divan. She clutched him to her breast and kissed him softly on his head.

Now it was James' turn to raise his voice. "Listen - listen to me, Mrs. Brown. Calm down. This is an opportunity which will never occur again. To have an image of Castor, together with his brother, captured as a photographic image for all eternity. You're in grief. I've seen many grief-stricken people, and often things are said that people don't mean."

Mrs. Brown's hyperventilating tantrum began to subside, and her excitability diminished.

"I know how important this is to you, Ma'am, and I have a suggestion. Let's take a break. Polux and I will go outside for some air, and you and your beloved Castor can be alone."

Mrs. Brown complied with James' suggestion. She embraced Castor, and sweetly whispered into his ear. Then James gestured to Polux to accompany him outside.

The two sat down on a lounge on the porch. The October sun bathed them in warmth and light.

"I'm so sorry, Polux. This experience has got to be a nightmare for you. If you would like to talk about it I can offer a sympathetic ear. Sometimes talking about our trials and tribulations can give us some degree of solace."

Polux's eyes were bathed in tears and he faltered as he spoke.

"It's worse. Worse than you can imagine. No nightmare could be as horrible as my life.

My mother killed Castor. She thought he was me. She has rages - violent rages. This time she went crazy with rage and forgot to look for the birthmark on my back. That birthmark is the only thing that makes Castor and me different."

He paused, wiping away tears and catching his breath. "There are people - neighbors - who speak in whispers, who believe my mother also killed my father because he objected to her mistreatment of me."

Polux held his face in his hands, then looked up to James. "Please help me, Mr. Hundly."

James felt sick - sick in his heart and soul. He could feel this hapless boy's pain. His own mother was often engulfed by moods of darkness and would lash out in cruelty. But it was nothing like this. Mrs. Brown had transcended the status of abusive parent and risen to the position of malignant, homicidal bitch.

James embraced Polux, then gently lifted his chin and smiled.

"I think I have a solution." He looked back toward the house, then returned his gaze to Polux. "I want you to stay here on the porch, and try to enjoy this beautiful October day. I'll go back inside for a brief meeting with your mother. I'm confident that the solution will result in what's best for everyone. Now relax until I come to get you. This shouldn't take long."

James walked into the house, and Polux looked about at his surroundings. He felt caressed by the day's warmth. Across the street a huge red maple tree bore leaves that glowed with crimson and yellow. If only this moment was not fleeting. If only things were…

James came outside. The tension from earlier was gone. He looked light and happy.

"Come inside with me, Polux."

Polux was frozen with trepidation. "But - but my mother. She…"

James interrupted him. "Just come inside. Don't be afraid. I think you'll be pleased."

They went inside and walked into the parlor. Polux stopped in his tracks. He was not sure if what he saw before him was real.

On the divan his mother sat next to Castor, their bodies touching. Castor's hand lay on his mother's lap, enveloped by her hands. They looked beatific. Mother and son, basking beneath a halo of bliss. He never imagined his mother could look so happy and at peace.

"I don't do this sort of thing often," said James. "We can relax now and take our time."

He smiled, happy in his work, the work in which he took such pride. "All we need now is just a bit of emulsifier to cover the markings on her neck. Then I'll take the picture. It should be one of my best."

He bent behind the camera, his head beneath

the hood. Slowly, the image came into focus. Yes, it was perfect.

Especially her eyes, opened wide, brimming with mother love, staring forever into the void.

The Tonsorial Masterpiece

"He always spoke so highly of you. As you know, for the last ten years he wouldn't let anyone but you so much as touch his hair."

Jake Davis listened with quiet respect to Leonard Gellin's widow Martha. It was less than two days since Leonard had passed.

Jake thought about Leonard, and he thought about his own career as a barber.

There was something ritualistic and intimate about cutting another man's hair. From the moment the sheet is placed over the customer and the barber chair's height adjusted, a relationship began. It was one of the few contexts in which one man touches another where sex, violence, or stigma are not a factor.

And then there was trust. Holding a straight razor over another man's jugular during a shave was an act of trust, if indeed not faith. A steady hand and an eye for irregularities - moles, scar tissue, hypersensitive skin; any or all of these required finesse to make small adjustments in the pressure of the stroke. Jake had given thousands of shaves in his twenty years of barbering, all with nary a nick.

But another kind of trust was involved with haircuts. Every man fortunate to have hair had a clear visualization of how his hair should look. The really good barbers would listen closely to the customers' verbalizing that vision like a priest listening to a confession. The really good barbers could bring the customers' vision to tangible fruition with near perfection. Jake was an exceptional barber and could achieve total perfection.

Some of Jake's customers were chatterboxes; others were laconic, speaking as if there were a fee charged for every word spoken.

Leonard was one of the silent ones. "Hello Jake," he would say as he sat down on the barber's chair. And then, with rare exception, not another word until his haircut was finished. But when he was handed the mirror for final approval, he beamed. "Jake," he would say, "You've done it again - another tonsorial masterpiece!" Then he would leave a seventy percent tip.

"Jake," continued Martha, "it's explicit in his will. You will be paid handsomely. I'm afraid my dear Leonard could never rest in peace if you didn't give him his final haircut."

It was a warm, dry October day as Jake drove to the mortuary. Along the way small dust devils swirled, as if alive, only to disappear in the blink of an eye.

He knew almost nothing about Leonard - not his occupation, his background, his interests and hobbies, if indeed he had any. Had he not been contacted by his widow Martha, he would not have known that Leonard was even married. Jake only knew that Leonard approved of his haircuts, but he never would have conceived his approval was so strong that he insisted on going to the grave with a fresh cut. For Jake, this was an honor, and an honor that bore an extreme responsibility. Leonard could never rest in peace, Martha had emphatically said, without a final haircut by Jake.

It was late morning when he arrived at the Treach Family Mortuary. Before getting out of his car he double checked the barber tools in his satchel: shears, scissors, razors, comb, clippers, mirror, and lotions - all there. The mirror, he realized, would of course not be necessary. Leonard would hardly be in a state in which he could voice approval, but better to prepare for all exigencies. A barber giving a dead man a haircut lent itself to the sardonic.

As he stepped out of his car, a police squad car pulled up beside him. A tall, burly plainclothes officer approached Jake. He had sandy hair and appeared to be in his early fifties. His face reflected a lifetime of distrust and cynicism.

When he spoke he was polite but officious. "Hello sir. Are you Jake Davis?"

"Why, yes officer, I am. How can I help you?"

"It's a bit hot out here," replied the officer. "Let's go inside to the mortuary's lobby, where it should be much cooler and we can sit. I'd like to ask you a few questions."

They went inside and approached the young man at the front desk. "Hello - I'm homicide investigator Detective Robert Stern, and this gentleman is Jake Davis. Mr. Davis has been requested to give one of your guests, a Mr. Leonard Gellin, a haircut before his burial. Would you mind if Mr. Davis and I have a chat in the lobby? It's much more comfortable inside with your air conditioning than outdoors. It seems we're having an Indian summer heat wave a bit late this year; October normally begins a cooling trend. I hate to think of what an establishment like this would be like during a heat wave prior to the advent of central cooling and refrigeration." Stern paused. He tried to smile but could only manage a grimace. "I imagine your guests would be encouraged not to overstay their welcome."

If the young man appreciated Stern's humor, he was adept at concealing it. His expression was dour as he led the two men to a sofa in the lobby.

Jake sat on the sofa as Stern moved a chair in front of him so they could converse face to face. The cool air was refreshing. Jake looked about. There was nothing in the lobby to suggest they were in a mortuary aside from the stained glass windows. Off to the side there was a fountain. The gentle sound of babbling water lent to an atmosphere of tranquility.

"Tell me, Mr. Davis. What did you know of Leonard Gellin? Did he ever mention anything disturbing or unusual while you cut his hair?"

"Why no, Detective. In fact, we rarely spoke at all. He was, however, always complimentary of my work and would show his appreciation with a generous tip."

Detective Stern studied Jake as he spoke. He had risen in the ranks quickly due to his analytical skills and keen observation. His colleagues often joked that he was a human polygraph machine and could tell if someone was lying within seconds. He quickly decided that Jake was no liar.

"Mr. Davis, Leonard Gellin had been a person of interest in a series of crimes for many years."

"Crimes," Jake responded." Leonard? What kind of crimes?"

Stern looked at Jake. His eyes and demeanor were stone cold.

"We've gathered a substantial amount of forensic evidence that Leonard Gellin, during the last fifteen years, had murdered at least eleven people - perhaps more. Had he not died he would be in custody as we speak. It was only last week that we finally established a DNA link between him and his victims. We're certain, Mr. Davis, beyond any reasonable doubt, that Gellin was a serial murderer."

Jake nearly went into shock. Leonard? He always appeared so meek and harmless - the kind of man who could not harm a fly - even if he wanted to, let alone multiple murders.

"Have you spoken with his wife Martha?"

"Yes, we have, Mr. Davis. At length. The poor woman. First her husband dies, then the authorities inform her that he was a serial killer. She couldn't suspend disbelief and became hysterical. We're confident she knows nothing about her husband's secret life, which is not unusual. It's almost cliché that serial killers are quiet, withdrawn people, described as perfect neighbors."

"How… How did Leonard die? Martha didn't say when I spoke with her."

"Heart attack. Sudden and massive. Well, it looks like the Grim Reaper got to him before we could. He was a clever bastard, your appreciative customer. He knew how to sanitize his handiwork. Getting the DNA was like finding a needle in a haystack. Well, it looks like eleven homicide cases will go cold - with asterisks.

That should do it, Mr. Davis. Do a good job on Gellin. We wouldn't want him to be poorly coiffed in Hell."

As Stern walked away, Jake had a final question. "By the way, detective. What was Leonard's line of work? I always wondered."

Without pausing or turning around, Stern shouted to Jake. "Insurance. He sold life insurance."

Jake returned to his car and retrieved his satchel of barber tools. He was shaken as he returned to the mortuary and approached the front desk. Jake was confident the young man had not overheard any of his conversation with Stern.

"And where can I find Mr. Gellin?" he asked the young man.

"Straight down the hall and to the right," he replied. "Room 121."

He placed his hand on the door handle. It felt like ice. Then he opened the door and went inside.

Leonard was lying supine on a metal table. He was covered from the neck down with a white sheet. Jake walked over to the table and looked at Leonard in repose. He appeared neither dead nor alive, but in a neutral state, almost as if he were waiting for his haircut before he could fully release himself from the earthly realm.

Jake opened his satchel and was startled by a voice. "Hello - you must be Mr. Davis." Jake turned around and was met by a slender man with thinning hair wearing hospital scrubs.

"My name is Gordon Dexter. I'm the senior mortician here at Treach Family." He extended his arm and he and Jake shook hands. Dexter's hand felt cold and moist, and the entire room felt as if it were an icy chamber. What should he expect - a sauna? Rooms such as this were cold for a purpose.

"Well, Mr. Davis, I suppose you would like to get started?" Perhaps against stereotype, Dexter was a jovial and gracious man.

"We've customized a few things in consideration of your task." Dexter pressed a button below the table. There was a soft humming sound as Leonard's torso began to rise to nearly a ninety-degree angle. "We sadly could not provide you with a barber's chair, but hopefully this is a reasonable facsimile. Now, let me leave you to the task at hand, Maestro."

Jake set to work. He was expecting the experience would be macabre or unnerving, but such was not the case. It felt normal - just like old times. The fact of the matter is, Leonard always assumed a corpse-like appearance, barely moving and speaking ever so briefly before and after the haircut. He looked at Leonard's face. He bore the same static expression he assumed while alive, showing neither joy nor displeasure. His cheeks and forehead were a bit shiny, but Jake attributed that to the mortician's wax.

He began. Wielding his shears and scissors like a classical music conductor, the tapered fade pompadour that Leonard preferred began to take form. Jake was in his glory; he remembered Michaelangelo's comment that the great statue of David was already formed, lying dormant within the block of marble, and it was merely a matter of chiseling away the excess in order to reveal the masterpiece. Before he even touched his shears and scissors, Jake could visualize the perfect haircut for both Leonard's and his own standard; a lofty, ethereal standard that reflected not just the perfect haircut, but indeed the essence of haircutness itself.

And so it was. Within twenty minutes, the perfect tapered fade pompadour burst forth from an amorphous mass of follicles just as David burst forth from his marble prison.

He stepped back from what he had wrought. The haircut was beyond perfect - it was sublime.

Was it force of habit or an expression of unconscious grim humor? Without thinking, Jake held the mirror for Leonard's approval. Though in no condition to vocalize, he felt that Leonard was fully satisfied wherever he may be.

The following day, Jake had an assistant run the shop so he could attend Leonard's service and funeral.

When he arrived, he noticed how few people

were gathered in the chapel. There was of course Martha and a smattering of others Jake guessed to be her friends and family. It appeared that Leonard was alone in the world save for Martha. She seemed to be a decent woman and must have seen some positive qualities in Leonard. Jake scanned the chapel for others. Incongruously, detective Stern sat in the back row.

The pastor said a few words - a very few words. Perfunctory, cliché, and boilerplate words. Martha appeared stoic, showing little by way of grief and sorrow.

The small assemblage walked by Leonard's open casket. No one gave more than a cursory glance as they passed except the last person in line-detective Stern. He paused and stared intently at Leonard, then, with a slight sardonic smile, moved on.

The casket was closed and six burly pallbearers who Jake assumed were mortuary employees carried the casket outside to the gravesite.

As the small group followed, Jake approached detective Stern. "Hello detective Stern. If you don't mind my saying, you're the last person in the world I would expect to see here. May I ask why?"

"Of course you may ask. It's curiosity. I wanted to see his hair. You've exceeded my expectations, Mr. Davis. His hair is, quite simply, perfect."

"Thank you, Detective. Thank you very much indeed. And one final question if I may."

"Of course, you may. I'm in no hurry. Such a beautiful October day - a perfect day for a funeral."

"Well, Detective, do you have any doubt, even the very slightest, that Leonard murdered those people?"

Stern looked at Jake, his expression cold and solemn. "None, Mr. Davis - absolutely none. I'm as certain as if I were an actual eyewitness. And I'm equally certain that although Leonard Gellin's body is in a box, right now, as we speak, his soul is burning in Hell."

Stern shook Jake's hand, then turned and walked toward his car. Jake looked at Leonard's gravesite in the near distance. The casket had already been lowered in the grave and covered. The assemblage had departed for home, including Martha.

Jake felt a need to give Leonard a last farewell. After all, he had been Jake's most loyal and appreciative customer. And Stern was not infallible; death row was notorious for containing innocent people.

He walked to the gravesite. The head stone was stark, bearing only Leonard's name and dates of birth and death. "Goodbye, Leonard," he whispered. "Rest in peace."

On impulse, he wanted to leave something for Leonard that spoke of their relationship. He walked back to his car to retrieve his satchel, then returned to the gravesite.

It was growing dark as Jake reached into his satchel for his favorite straight razor - the one with the scrimshaw handle. He placed it on Leonard's grave, then left for home.

It had been a long day. Jake removed his suit coat as he entered his house and tossed the satchel on the bed. It popped open on impact, and Jake looked at the contents spilling out. The scrimshaw razor was still there. In the darkness, back at the cemetery, he had mistaken one of his cheaper razors, the one with a white plastic handle, for the special one.

It was growing late, but not too late. He zipped up the satchel and threw it over his shoulder. The cemetery was just a few miles away. He felt compelled to drive back and correct the error he had made.

When he arrived at the cemetery, it was nearing midnight. Enough moonlight remained in the sky to make the path to Leonard's grave navigable.

He stood before the headstone. The plastic handled razor was where he left it. As he bent to retrieve it, he heard a sound.

It sounded like a voice. No, numerous voices, a muffled chorus as if spoken from a deep well.

What were the voices saying? Then they became clearer. They were calling out to him.

"Help us Jake - we need you." Then another voice. "Don't leave us, Jake - stay with us."

The voices were coming up from beneath the ground; a macabre litany of urgent, pleading voices - coming up from the graves. Then, there was silence, except for one clear and familiar voice. It was the voice of Leonard.

"A tonsorial masterpiece indeed, Jake - perhaps the best you've ever done. And that opinion is unanimous."

Jake tried to keep his wits. This was not real. This must be a nightmare.

"I've made some fast friends down below but, alas, none of them are perfect as you might expect of the residents of Hell. As soon as I arrived, they revealed their jealousy. It's my hair, Jake - they covet my hair.

Come, Jake. Descend. Ease the torment of these wretched souls - and my soul. Be the barber for us all - for eternity."

He looked down. Hands were erupting from the ground. They were everywhere, grasping at his legs and ankles, dragging and tugging at him.

The descent began. The earth was cold above the fire below. He screamed. Then he was gone.

He was now, literally, the best damned barber ever.

Author: Ron Terranova

Ron Terranova is a former Orange County Deputy Assessor. He began writing at age eleven after nearly dying of a serious illness. He is a graduate of California State University, Long Beach where he received a degree in English. He lives in Huntington Beach, California.

He is the author of the novel, "I, Polyphemus", and has had numerous poetry published, most recently in "Chiron Review". He is also a blogger (rterranova.com) and "October Twilight" is a sequel to his prior short story collection "October Light."

Also by Ron Terranova:

I, Polyphemus

Also by ReadLips Press:

Swimming Middle River
  by Leah Holbrook Sackett

How to Throw a Psychic a Surprise Party
  by Noreen Lace

www.ingramcontent.com/pod-product-compliance
Lightning Source LLC
Chambersburg PA
CBHW020907180626
46816CB00007BA/2282